So Great a Cloud of Witnesses

All the things I've written,
have been but fragments
of one long confession.
— GOETHE

So Great a Cloud of Witnesses

David O. Rankin

Strawberry Hill Press

Strawberry Hill Press   Distributed by Stackpole Books
616 44th Avenue   Cameron & Kelker Sts.
San Francisco, California 94121   Harrisburg, Pa. 17105

First Printing, March, 1978

Manufactured in the United States of America

Typesetting by Medallion Graphics, San Francisco

Book design by David Harrell

Library of Congress Cataloging in Publication Data

Rankin, David O   1938-
    So great a cloud of witnesses.

    Bibliography: p.
    1. Unitarian churches—Sermons.   2. Sermons,
American.   I. Title.
BX9843.R26S6   252'.08   78-2584
ISBN 0-89407-014-2

Dedication

To Virginia, who keeps my head in the clouds —
and to Mark, Oran and Jean, who keep my feet
firmly planted in the ground.

Acknowledgements

I am very grateful for the patience of the members and friends of the First Unitarian Church of San Francisco; for the personal encouragement of David Harrell; for the help and understanding of Virginia Rankin, who missed a vacation; and for the inspiration of all the Cloud of Witnesses who appear in the pages of this book.

DOR

Contents

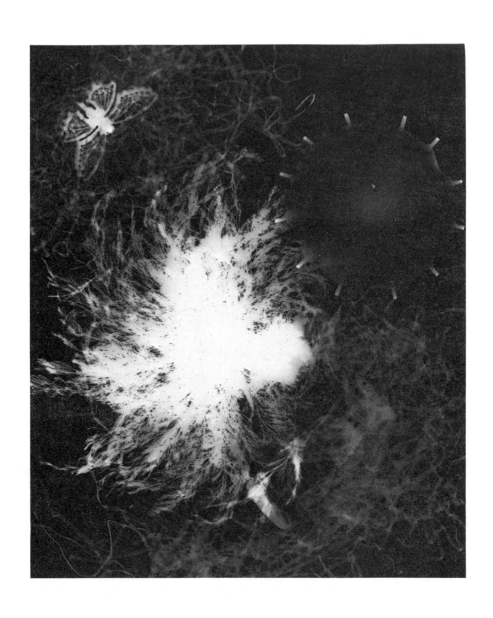

Preface

Preface

A View of the Author

None of the usual descriptions of a minister fit the Reverend David O. Rankin. How many ministers would claim authorship to sermons such as: "I Lost My Faith in Wheaties," or "A View From the Dump," or "Should I Swim to Honolulu?" Yet these are just a few of his more provocative sermons, many of which have moved the congregation to spontaneous applause since his arrival in San Francisco in 1973.

A tall, slender man in his late thirties, with a shock of silver at the temples, he is warm and outgoing — he radiates the feeling that he *really* cares about people. Usually wearing turtleneck-sportcoat combinations in the office, and occasionally in place of his black vestments in the pulpit, he cultivates an air of informality.

Since entering the ministry, he has survived physical assaults, as well as many threats upon his life. "In the urban church," he says, "a sense of humor (and speed) are indispensable." During one of his sermons, he sat on the floor next to the pulpit pretending to be Charlie Brown! He has also appeared as Judas, St. Peter, and Groucho Marx! His presentations are always carefully written, eclectic, and timely.

An insight into the inner feelings of the minister is revealed in one of his sermons:

> *Is there such a thing as God?*
> *I saw a sunrise at Jackson Hole.*
> *I fell in love many years ago.*
> *I saw a tear in my father's eye.*
> *I watched a lily bloom.*
> *I saved a boy from drugs and death.*
> *I touched the hand of Martin Luther King.*
> *I feel the warmth of children.*
> *I laugh almost every day.*
> *I hold the hem of hope.*
> *The only wisdom I can hope to acquire is the wisdom*
> *of humility — and humility is endless.*

As an instructor of Political Science at Cornell College in Iowa, David Rankin became dissatisfied with the academic life.

"I didn't want to be in just one discipline; I wanted more depth in teaching and in dealing with people of all ages."

After earning a Divinity Degree from Tufts University, he served two Unitarian-Universalist churches in Watertown and New Bedford, Massachusetts. He demonstrated his concern for people of all ages by actively participating in draft counseling, drug rehabilitation, reform of correctional institutions, and work with senior citizens. One of his sermons, "The Salvation of New Bedford," won the Clarence R. Skinner Award for the sermon most expressive of the Unitarian-Universalist social philosophy.

In his first sermon at the First Unitarian Church of San Francisco, David Rankin defined what the church is to him when he said:

So let me tell you of a lesson I have learned in the ministry —
I have learned not to take my position too seriously.
Or my image too seriously. Or myself too seriously.
I have learned that the most important item in the religious community is the people of the religious community.
And I have learned that the real church can be defined as our most intimate relationships —
How we smile and trust each other.
How we talk and touch each other.
How we share and protect each other.
How we welcome new friends and forgive old enemies.
How we love each other — in all the myriad ways that love can be expressed.
That is the church!

So I think you will enjoy this collection — written by a man who played basketball with Wilt Chamberlain; entertained Martin Luther King; officiated at the wedding of Red Skelton; preached on social action to Eldridge Cleaver — and who combines the playfulness, the compassion, the wit, and the anger of all. If you have never liked sermons, then this is the book you should read.

Jeanne Whitesell
Danville, California
1978

Chapter I
In The Beginning Was The Word

There Was a Child Went Forth

"There was a child went forth every day,
And the first object he looked upon, that object he became,
And that object became part of him for the day
or a certain part of the day –
Or for many years or stretching cycles of years."

I

The comfort of woman's milk became part of this child,
And the three-room apartment in the steel-mill town, and the
red-brick streets, and the belching clouds of smoke from the
tall thick fingers, and the bright orange sky at night, and
the silence of no birds singing.
And the street-car stopping at the light below, and the smell
of coke-sulphur-ore, and the clanging of the train rushing
to feed the monstrous galaxy of ovens-pits-tubes, and the
noisy grinding of gear on gear — pushing, pulling, pulsing.
And the black snow falling from heaven in July,
And the soft food spooned in the mouth,
And the wet bed in the evening,
And the cries and tears of revenge,
All became part of him.

II

And the long, thin body became part of him.
And the brown hair, and the soft teeth, and the strong legs, and
the stammering speech which led to early shyness.
And the wonderful names of neighbors — Eggenloff, Showerball,
and Bumgardener — Markovich, Krajack, and Danko —
Kerensky, Kantakis, and Petrulli.
And the old drunk lying on the curb on payday,

9

And the friendly boys who played, and the quarrelsome boys
    who fought,
And the rich girls in the shiny cars with automatic windows,
And the poor girls with legs for walking and lips for kissing,
And all the changes of city and soul wherever he went.

III

His own parents, he that had fathered him and she that had con-
    ceived him in her womb and nurtured him,
They gave this child more of themselves than that,
        for they gave him afterward every day, and they became
        part of him.
The mother at home quietly dusting the dining room table with
    a mind far distant — and the mother not at home — at
    church, or club, or party.
The mother neat, proud, impatient — a social being with the
    energy of lightning — clapping, bursting, thundering — and
    seething at the core.
The father strong, soft, angry, kind, unjust, tender — the hours
    of silence, the quick loud word, the blow, the bargain, and
    all forgotten.
The father at work breathing the dust of America's greatness,
    and the father at home — coughing, choking, spitting —
    for the U.S.A.
The family traditions, the secret language, the company of rela-
    tives, the furniture, and the older brother with first choice
    on the double-deck bed,
All of that became part of him.

IV

And the yearning and troubled heart, that too became part of him.
The sense of what is real, and the thought if after all it should
    prove unreal,
And the doubts of daytime, and the doubts of night-time, and
    the curious whether and how:
        Whether that which appears so is so, or is it all flashes
           and specks?
        Whether the hollow knees and elbows will ever fill with
           skin and flesh?
        Whether all Chesterfields are as foul as the first?
        And whether all sex is lonely and forbidden?
        And whether God can see in the dark?

And whether death is going to reap the father, the
    mother, brother, himself? Certainly not himself!
And all the thoughts and fears wherever he went.

V

The culture of the era became part of this child.
The Saturday matinee with the Marx Brothers at the Opera,
    and Johnny Mack Brown, and Boris Karloff, and Rita Hay-
    worth — and stomping in unison when the projector failed.
And the pornography under the socks, under the hankies, under
    the newspaper, in the left-hand corner of the top dresser
    drawer.
And the first raw taste of beer at Pulaski Grove, with the odor
    of polish sausage and the strains of a polka preceding the
    dizziness.
And the reefer smoking under the porch,
And Joe Louis beating Billy Conn in every place but Pittsburgh,
And white bucks, and tapered pants, and padded shoulders, and
    a long black comb, and an ego too wide for a pork-pie hat,
And all the dreams and fantasies wherever he went.

VI

And the struggle for survival became part of him.
The mass of men and women crowding in the streets — indistin-
    guishable grays and blacks — hurrying, tumbling, slapping,
    scratching for a place in the sun.
That day in the park — bright sunlight, banks of red and blue
    flowers, weeping willow trees, the grass is very green — and
    there is no guilt, only the splash and splatter of the water
    in the fountain.
And the gravelled paths in twelve directions, and no one to tell
    him which to take, and he can take any one of the paths, and
    he is free, and he can choose, and he has to choose, and a
    whole new life has begun.
And the silly phantom bouncing basketballs for the pleasure
    of the crowd,
And dealing cards in school yards, and shooting dice in alleys,
    to mark him from the ants and sparrows — unique in his
    creation.
And wanting to be needed, to be necessary, to be somebody —
All became part of him.

VII

The horizon's edge became part of him, of what to be or not
to be.
How molten ingots burn the flesh — and time clocks kill the
spirit,
How garbage cans make crooked backs — and ankles ache on
hardwood floors,
How teeth are lost to human fists — and derelicts age too early.
That night in the ring — bright lights, banks of black and white
faces, hanging lifeless arms, the blood is very red — and
there is no victory, only the moaning and the cheering of
the voices in the hall.
And the wooden steps in two directions, and no one to tell him
which to take, and he can take either one of the steps, and
he is free, and can choose, and he has to choose, and a whole
new life has begun.
And the cum laude graduate of three universities bouncing the
tassels of his cap to the pleasure of the crowd,
And the retiring professor in the halls of ivy teaching for fame
and poverty,
And all the books and journals wherever he went.

VIII

And the love of the world became part of this child.
Shadows, fog and mist, the light falling on ocean waves, mountains, the fragrance of flower and desert,
And the splendid isolation of Coeur d'Alene, the rich black earth
of Keokuck, and the rocky desolation of North New York,
and the gabled mansions of ancient sea captains,
And the woman — brown hair, round eyes, soft face — the
woman at home in heat or cold — the woman strong, sage,
original — forgetful of keys, pocketbook, and clocktime —
and mindful only of love, trust, and promises of long ago,
And children gained through agencies — one small and slight,
with half his body heart — one tall and thin and goofy-like,
with dreams as large as stars — and one that's round and
beautiful, with a spirit of her own,
And cherry trees covered with blossoms, and the big bing
cherries, and the redwood forests, and the commonest
weeds by the road —
All became part of him.

IX

And the gift of faith became part of him.

Faith in the presence of God — though in the midst of anguish
and despair,

And faith in the power of good over evil, and faith in the value
of honest prayer, and faith that one mistake will always
lead to another — until the virtue of humility is at last
attained.

That day in the study — bright glare, banks of thin and thick
books, listless absent mind, the brain is very full — and
there is no knowledge, only the chatter of a million quotations in an empty coffee cup,

And the rugged path in one direction, and no one to tell him to
take it, and he can take it if he wants, and he is free, and
he can choose, and he has to choose, and a whole new life
has begun.

And the nimble minister bouncing ancient scriptures off the old
church walls,

And the liberal clergyman sparring with the demons of the day,

And all the thousand "thees" wherever he went.

X

And the cries of human misery became part of this child.

The frozen pleas in nursing homes, and the wail of mourners,
the hollow screams of jails and prisons, and the morbid
murmur of an addict singing,

And the police cars screeching at the light below, and the smell
of drugs-death-booze, and the whining of the ambulance
to feed the insatiable cells-rooms-wards, and the patterned
ticking of computers — whirring, stuttering, snooping,

And the rain falling on a soldier's grave,

And a child crushed by a Cadillac,

And the wet tears in the evening,

And the cry and rage of helplessness,

All became part of him.

XI

And hope became part of him.

Hope seen in the spring sprouts, and those of the light yellow
corn, and the firm roots of the garden,

And hope gleaned from the lips of martyrs, and the song of angels on Christmas Eve, and the moonbeams dancing in the eyes of an infant,

And hope found in the struggle of the salmon, and in the peace following a storm, and in the everlasting hilarity of W.C. Fields,

And hope flowing from an evening's whisper,

And hope forged from a frenzied prayer,

And hope captured in the smiles of known companions who help along the way,

All these became part of that child, who went forth every day, and who now goes, and will always go forth every day, or for many years, or stretching cycles of years.

"and nothing quite so least as truth —
I say though hate were why men breathe —
because my father lived his soul
love is the whole and more than all"
— e. e. cummings

Honor Thy Father

When I was eight years old, he hit me in the face with a pork chop for talking back to his wife. But he was the most gentle man I have ever known.

When I was nine years old, he encouraged me to learn to defend myself on the streets. But he could always wrestle me to the ground with one arm.

When I was ten years old, I informed him that I was going to run away from home. He offered to buy me a bus ticket, and told me to take a winter jacket.

When I was eleven years old, he announced it was time I work for a living. Over the years, I worked as a golf-ball retriever, a bathhouse boy, a garbageman, a laborer, and a toy salesman. But he never recommended a particular career.

When I was twelve years old, he said we were going to Santiago, Chile, where he had been offered a position in a new steel mill. But I lived in the same house for over twenty years, and never left the state of Pennsylvania.

When I was fifteen years old, he presented the first and only lecture on sex education. It consisted of one brief sentence, somewhat muffled, unspeakably graphic, and forever useful.

When I was eighteen years old, he shook my hand and sent me off to college. I was thereafter known as one of those "God damn college kids!"

When I was twenty years old, he told me I could own my own car — if I bought it with my own money, paid all the bills, and promised not to cruise around.

When I was twenty-one years old, he took me to his favorite tavern and bought me a beer. We talked about baseball and politics, but never returned.

When I was twenty-two years old, he fell in love with my

bride, slipped me five hundred dollars, and warned me to be kind.

When I was twenty-three years old, he wrote me a letter on the Presidential Election. It was one of the few times he ever asked me a real question — or sought my advice.

A few months later he died.

I never knew him well, but he was my father.

The Scots-Irish have no roots. I have often envied the Irish, the Germans, the Yankees, the Afro-Americans, who are able to trace their lineage, to take pride in their ancestry, and to enter into the spirit of their history.

For the Scots-Irish, though characterized by sturdy integrity and physical vigor on the one hand, and by stiffness and rigidity of temperament on the other, have no common historical identity and little interest in one another.

They are neither shrewd like the Yankees and the Scots; nor practical like the English and the Swedes; nor philosophical like the Germans and the French; nor artistic like the Japanese and the Africans; nor clannish like the Italians and the Chinese. No, the Scots-Irish just seem to exist, and usually on the borders of civilization, as isolated individualists. Though often found in cities, they live like Eskimos.

In response to a child's curiosity, my father always replied that his ancestors "were a bunch of horsethieves, who disappeared with the invention of the automobile." And while I desperately tried to connect our family heritage to Representative Rankin in Montana, or to Senator Rankin in Mississippi, or to John Rankin, the famous abolitionist preacher in Ohio — he always claimed there were more Rankins in any Boot Hill than in the Hall of Fame. It was a peculiar kind of pride.

Of course, behind the humor was tragedy. My father was born in the year 1900 in the Tenth Ward of McKeesport, Pennsylvania. It was known as "Shacktown" at the time, because the homes were flimsy structures used by those who were employed by the railroad or steel mill. They were much like the homes of the Chicanos in the West today.

His mother's name was Rose, a patient, long-suffering woman who would die of exhaustion and disease at an early age. His father's name was seldom mentioned in our home, and it would be many years before I learned that he had been an active alcoholic who had mistreated his wife and children, squandered an inheritance, and was constantly in debt. It was broadly rumored that on one cold, wintry evening he was run over by a train while sleeping on the track. I have often heard conflicting stories, though none are noble.

In any event, my father was sixteen years old when he dropped out of school to support his mother and sister. He began as a waterboy for the United States Steel Corporation, where he remained for the final forty-four years of his life. They gave him a watch "For 40 years of loyal and faithful service." I wear it today as a token of esteem for him — and as a token of dislike for them.

Over the years, there was a remarkable marriage to a remarkable woman and three boisterous sons. There were wars and depressions. There were union battles, strikes, and lock-outs. But mostly, it was 12 daily hours of grinding labor: lifting steel by hand in the Rolling Mill, choking on the gas at the Soaking Pit, and living amidst the awful dirt, the deafening noise, and the constant danger of America's greatest industry.

So if he did not fully develop the social graces, it was because his life had been cruelly interrupted by the simple necessity of survival.

If he did not display the normal outward affection toward his children, it was because he, himself, had never known such a father.

If he never attended church on Sunday mornings, it was because the clergy did not relate to his own personal anguish and daily concern.

If he did not respect intellectuals (and he despised them with a passion), it was because they looked upon him as a mere number, a statistic, an abstraction.

If he did not trust the new-style leaders of the union, it was because they were then wearing the white shirts, ties, and business suits of the old enemy.

If he did not quite believe in the American Dream, it was because he detected that the success of others was always at his expense.

And, if he liked to sit at home on the porch at night, lost in the silence of his own private world — it was because it was HIS home, and HIS porch, and HIS world.

But, I never knew him well.

In the year of my sixteenth birthday, I was told to report to the United States Steel Corporation for summer employment. I worked there for the next four summers, as a sweeper, a laborer, and a driller — long enough to learn that breaking a book is easier than breaking a back — a lesson arranged for just that purpose!

One day, I remember, I was walking down a ramp in the mill, when I passed a huge black man. I noticed, printed on his hat, the letters: "ORAN." So I stopped the stranger, and said something stupid, like: "What an unusual name you have!" But he laughed and replied: "The big man upstairs gave me his old hat, and it's the only white man's hat I'd ever wear!" Of course, "the big man upstairs" was dad.

The mill was an education. One of the assumptions about the working class, accentuated by the popularity of TV's Archie Bunker, is that blue-collar workers represent everything that is backward and reprehensible in American society. It is an assumption of the intellectual sons and daughters of the Middle Class, a latent prejudice of liberals and radicals. It has little to do with reality.

For I knew a workingman who never uttered an unkind word against minority people. He jeopardized his own personal promotions through supporting the rights of minorities to management positions. He was a prime mover for the hiring of the first black foreman in the mill. He consistently encouraged the Puerto Ricans in their struggle with both union and company.

I knew a workingman who was completely devoid of male chauvinism. He shopped for the food on Saturday afternoon and always cooked the Sunday dinner. He helped clear the table, wash the dishes, and clean the kitchen. Not once did he ever speak down to women, or treat them with anything other than respect.

And yet I knew a workingman who was tough and hard. When a slightly retarded laborer was verbally assaulted by a Superintendent, he entered the argument, pinned the executive against the wall, and threatened to relocate several of his vital organs. I watched him one day, during my lunch hour, push a union official through a door and off a loading platform. He described it later as "exercise."

To be sure — I could never fully understand all of the conflicting passions, the contradictory expressions, or the paradoxical behavior, but then again — I never knew him well.

The last time I had an extended conversation with my father was a year before his death. He asked me if I had learned anything after studying Political Science for four years. And even though I knew that his questions were never questions (but veiled threats for the purpose of opening a spirited argument), I took the bait. I replied that I had learned a great deal about the political system, and that I intended to try to change it. He responded with: "BLANK-blank" — with just that emphasis.

He went on to say: "People out there (pointing vaguely into the dark) don't give a damn about your theories.

"They want you to be reliable. They want you to be honest. They want you to be fair. They may even want you to be brave. But a theory and a nickel will not even get you a cup of coffee.

"You're a smart boy, Dave, but you're dumb as hell."

I admit, it was not much for a final memory. But it was typical of the man. I never won an argument. I never even finished an argument!

It was a subtle relationship — our life together. We never went skiing, sailing, or to a fancy French restaurant. Yet I was never deprived. In a thousand ways:

A blanket covering my chest at night —

A heavy hand on the back of my head —

A favorite meal prepared —

A certain look in his eyes —

A silent pride —

A trusting glance —

in a thousand ways was love conveyed. Of course, I never knew him well.

It is good to honor our fathers — but we will *never* know them well. Not only are they hidden from us by a multitude of years lived prior to our births, but also by secrets of sorrow, and of fear, and of striving that we will never comprehend.

It is meaningful to explore the hidden pools, the shrouded mysteries, and the shadows of their existence — for it tells us much about ourselves. But in the end, when we have probed as deep as we can or care to go, we must always say: "I never knew him well."

"Some beliefs are like shadows, darkening
children's days with unknown calamities.
Other beliefs are like sunshine, blessing
children with the warmth of happiness."
— SOPHIA FAHS

I Lost My Faith in Wheaties

It was a day of absolute infamy!

Perhaps you remember. It was the day Mr. Robert B. Choate Junior, an expert on hunger and nutrition, announced that most American breakfast cereals are nutritional frauds. In low and menacing terms he said: "They represent empty calories, and produce nothing but fat."

It was a brutal statement, which elicited only a mild reaction from the non-breakfast-food-eating world. The scrambled eggs and bacon people, the french toast and coffee crowd, the juice and sausage freaks, and the natural food contingent all smiled knowingly over the morning papers, with no charity or compassion for those of us in the cereal community.

But I was disturbed. In fact, I was profoundly shocked! I experienced an ontological anxiety — an insecurity about the ultimate foundations of the universe. And why not?

No Christian mystic ever looked forward to divine union more than I looked forward to each new box of Wheaties.

No Tibetan monk was ever devoted to the ritual of meditation more than I was devoted to the ritual of eating cereal.

And no Unitarian was ever driven to reform the world more than I was driven by the promises on the cereal box.

It was shattering! So let me explain.

Looking back, now, over thirty years, I can still recall how a summer day began. I woke, slipping on my Keds and Levi's, and moving silently past my sleeping brothers. I descended to the stairs and darted to the cupboard, to choose between Wheaties, Shredded Wheat, Pep, or something else of masculine promise. Not the current effete offering of Twinkies, Frosty O's, and Krinkles!

21

I then slurped my cereal while intently studying the bright front of the cereal package. The large glass bowl on the cover (I could never see through my own bowl), the fresh fruit topping the cereal (I had never tasted a real strawberry), and the magnificent colors to brighten my day (I had not yet discovered Norman Rockwell).

Then the back panel of the package, as I munched the second bowl. The pictures of Joe DiMaggio, Ralph Kiner, and other god-like athletes whose bulging muscles only hinted at what I might be.

And the box top. For only two coupons and ten cents — "a compass ring, with a secret compartment and a hidden can opener."

And finally, during the third bowl, the side panels of the package. Parents thought that no child read the technical nutritional data, but I memorized every chart. One ounce of cereal gave me one thousand per cent of the day's requirement of riboflavin, eight hundred per cent of the niacin, three hundred per cent of the iron, and on and on and on. Nutritional hoax? Empty calories? Nothing but fat? No, indeed! Not as the infallible, inerrant, inspired words on the box would have it!

So, after three bowls, I was prepared to confront the world. After all, I was filled with nine times the percentage of minimum daily adult requirements . . . and I was not even an adult!

I grabbed my glove. I met my friends. We went to the field. The game began. I came to bat. I struck out!

But do you think I blamed the cereal? Do you think my faith was shaken? Not at all! It was only that I had not eaten enough (or the pitcher had eaten more) — and the next day, with four bowls, everything would be different.

Thus, the revelations of Mr. Choate were profoundly shocking. Now, in the early morning hours, I sit eating my cereal — I mean, how could I ever give it up? — half believer, half agnostic, half atheist. Yes, I still read the charts on the box, but the scientific testimony floods my mind, and I am left as on a darkling plain.

It was the prophet Jeremiah who lamented: "Is it nothing to you, all you who pass by? Look and see if there is any sorrow like my sorrow. Hear how I groan? There is none to comfort me."

But alas, the pain of disillusionment knows no comfort. To the child, as to the adult, it is the most searing pain of all. And in the end, after all the packages are open, after all the prizes are received, after all the fantasies are gone, in the end, each of us murmurs the question (if only to ourselves): "Is nothing real? Is nothing real?"

I ask you to consider the example of a typical man. He is from a working class family. He is college educated. He is forty years of age. As he looks back upon his past and the evolution of his life, he sees the ruins of innumerable idols, the end of countless fantasies, and the entire record of disillusionment laid out before him. Here are his memories:

Age 1 – Warm house, warm clothes, warm bath, warm milk.

Age 2 – Cold. Believe in sucking thumb. Like to throw objects. Father is God. Mother protects me from God. I am indestructible.

Age 5 – Broke ankle jumping from porch. Dad is dumb. Mom is dumb. I am going to marry Diane Hacker. Chuckie Showerball is my best friend.

Age 8 – Hate girls and teachers. Enjoy the church. Accept the Bible as written — God, Jesus, Heaven and Hell. I was an angel in the school play.

Age 12 – I doubt the Bible. Shed idea of Hell. Church is boring. I am suspicious of the new minister. Pretend to be sick for the school play.

Age 15 – Read the Bible as history and legend. Shed Jesus. Quit church. I have fixed ideas of good and evil. Prefer evil.

Age 17 – A period of slight confusion. Read Emerson and available pornography. Exalt the self. Hate the self. Who am I? It has been a terrible year.

Age 19 – Discover Bertrand Russell. Shed everything else.

Age 20 – Plunge into biology, psychology, anthropology, and bars. Doubt everything but scientific facts. Religion is a crutch. Believe in free love — and the Pill.

Age 21 – Have doubts about the pill. I think women are inferior. Chuck and Diane have married. Despise the average person.

Age 23 – Embrace politics. Radicalism, confrontation, and no compromise. The state is the enemy of the people. The church is the opiate of the people. All power to the people!

Age 25 – Begin to suspect the people. See the need for a deeper revolution. My wife, Virginia, is exhausted. I will now have to work for a living. Enter teaching.

Age 27 – Talk. Listen to talk. More talk. Get tired. A great weariness. Sick of talk. Turn to philosophy and religion. Enter the ministry.

Age 32 – I believe in God, Heaven, social action, and the Annual Pledge Drive. J. Edgar Hoover is not a Unitarian. Good memories of my parents. Why do policemen look so young?

Age 37 – Three children. One sucks thumb. One hurt his ankle jumping from the porch. One likes to hit father with thrown objects. Warm house. Warm clothes. Warm bath. Warm milk.

Age 40 – What will I be tomorrow? Or this afternoon?

Of course, my example is not really typical. For we all grow in different ways, and move in many different directions. Yet we do share in the essential experience of looking back upon our lives and seeing the ghosts of past loyalties, the dust of old values, the ruins of innumerable gods, the debris of crushed hopes, and the wreckage wrought by disillusionment. For we have all wandered through time and space seeking a place to rest.

> *Through the dark oceans of the sky,*
> *Through the blue silences where no life breathes;*
> *Where time like a wind stirs and stirs the dust*
>   *of annihilated forms —*
>   *only to create new wholes.*

In San Francisco, there is a special awareness of the process of disillusionment as people are confronted daily by those who promise to end the journey. The city itself is a promise. It is a veritable trough of instant salvation. It is a city of faith, fad, and fable — of fraud, fool, and fanatic — of frill, froth, and fetish. I have been "saved" a hundred times in less than a year. The opportunities are endless — though shallow and lacking in permanence.

If you prefer a TRADITIONAL salvation — you can choose between Jehovah's Witnesses, the Mormons, Jews for Jesus, and the Billy Graham Crusade. There are three churches for every two people in San Francisco.

If you prefer a GLANDULAR salvation — you can choose between yoga exercises, communal living, massage parlors, and nude encounter groups. A streaker is inconspicuous in San Francisco.

If you prefer an ESOTERIC salvation — you can choose between astrology, transcendental meditation, Hare Krishna, and the comet Kohoutek. Science is banned in San Francisco.

If you prefer a CHARISMATIC salvation — you can choose between the Maharaj-Ji, Dr. Moon, Timothy Leary, and a large fruitcake of mystics, gurus, preachers and philosophers. There are more saviors than sinners in San Francisco.

And if you prefer a POLITICAL salvation — you can choose between the Progressive Labor Party, the SLA, the American Nazi Party, and the Mafia. Rhetoric is a separate language in San Francisco.

But the journey really never ends. There is no more truth in 'Frisco than in Poughkeepsie, Waterloo, or Nowhere, U.S.A.

For the legs of Witnesses get tired.
Billy Graham returns but once a year.
The communal kitchen burns the food.
The comet never does arrive.
Encounter groups are just like home.
The Maharaj-Ji likes his chocolate bars.
Dr. Moon's a Nixon man.
The gurus use their credit cards.
As for ESP and FBI, SLA and PSI, TA and POT —
one of them may hold the key, if you can pay
the entrance fee.

Illusions die hard — and it is painful.

Perhaps it is time to announce that to be human is to be involved in pain, in loss, in fear, in estrangement — in short, to be human is to lead a precarious and perilous existence. It means that one's very self is constantly menaced both from without and within by dark and destructive forces; it means living amidst the contradictions of good and evil; it means suffering confusion, loneliness, and despair. Suffering is real — and there is no cheap, or easy, or final exit. It is time to say it bluntly, for so many are being fooled.

I have no "ultimate" solutions. Indeed, the ultimate solutions are always as disappointing as a sign you see in a shop window, which reads: "Pressing Done Here." If you brought your clothes to be pressed, you would be fooled — for only the sign is for sale! It is better, I think, not to promise anything.

I have learned something in forty years.

> I have learned to trust those who are witnesses rather than gurus; those who express their confusion as well as their knowledge; those who share their suffering as well as their joy.

> I have learned that salvation is a life-long affair; that miracles are not often granted; that dreams are frequently smashed; that our hopes are never wholly attained.

> And I am learning how to deal with the long campaigns, the defeats, the dry seasons; how to suffer with my freedom; how to wrestle with my demons; how to love another; how to be gentle with myself.

But the end is only the beginning. My truths are not your truths, and we all have a long way to go.

In the remote mountains of northern India, there are numerous caves which people visit to find the key to faith and knowledge. In some of the caves there are gurus — burning incense, chanting, speaking pearls of wisdom. In other caves, there are saints and aesthetes — lying on beds of nails, chained to rocks, eating bugs and berries. And in still other caves, there are ancient manuscripts, magic relics, mysterious sounds, and prophetic inscriptions on the walls.

But in the most remote area of the mountains there is a smaller cave which all visitors are told to avoid. For when you arrive, and squeeze through the small entrance, and adjust your eyes to the darkness of the cave, and search expectantly for the key to faith and knowledge, there is nothing — nothing but a pool of water in which you see your own reflection.

Jock-Strap Theology

When I was a child, I could not relate to organized religion. It was either too cerebral — lost in heady intellectual abstractions; or it was too emotional — appealing to the lowest of human instincts. For a vigorous growing boy in Western Pennsylvania, eating juju beads in the back pew of the church on Sunday mornings, it was all too physically sterile.

I wondered why Moses never played hide-and-go-seek in the wilderness of Sinai;

I wondered why Confucius never learned ping-pong in the Chinese YMCA;

I wondered why Buddha never organized a volleyball league in populous India;

I wondered why Jesus never went swimming with his twelve dusty disciples;

and I wondered why Mohammed never practiced a broad-jump on the soft desert sand.

"How different from the pagan Greeks," I thought, "who extolled the physical attributes and worshipped the human body." If I had a God, it was Hermes: the son of Zeus; the Greek God of athletic contests; the merry cunning youth with winged hat and sandals. "To hell with all the others!"

Of course, I must admit that I pursued my God with a fanatical intensity known only to those who wish to escape from the steel-cities of Western Pennsylvania.

In the early years, my energies were consumed by games and contests. I participated in dodge-ball, kick the can, touch football, capture the flag, relay races, buck-buck,

27

billiards, vine swinging, and I even pitched pennies on
the corner at night to exercise my fingers — or so I said!
(Hermes was also the God of gambling.)

In the later years, my energies were concentrated on basketball. I played in the morning, afternoon, and evening.
Chipping ice from the ground in the winter, and broiling
in the heat of summer, was all part of the grueling ritual
— or so I thought! (Hermes was also the conductor of
souls to Hades.)

In the meantime, I paid no attention to the academic requirements of becoming a human being — and I graduated 443rd in
a class of 712. When I received my diploma, I stood in line with
the non-English speaking immigrants and the inmates of the
County Jail.

I suppose my greatest thrill in high-school was playing
against Wilt "the Stilt" Chamberlain, who still holds the career
scoring record in professional basketball. It was seen on television!

Before the game our coach said: "Dave, I want you to
guard Chamberlain. Push him around — and let him
know he's in a ball game!"

By which you have to understand, that in the lexicon of athletic
competition, the coach was really saying: "Dave, we're up against
this monster who's 7'2" tall, 290 pounds, and averaging 72 points
a game. Since you're expendable, go out and make him mad!"
It was not reassuring.

But I learned a great deal that day.

I learned that when you go up in the air with a fellow
who is twelve inches taller, your head and face are
exactly parallel to his elbows.

I learned that when you hold on to the shorts of a man
who is 125 pounds heavier, the laws of physics will
carry you through infinite space.

I learned that when you purposely step on the finger of
a giant who is momentarily sprawled on the floor,
you had better be prepared to find the beanstalk.

In any event, one of the great achievements of my life was "holding" Wilt Chamberlain to 55 points, and later winning the State
Championship with a minimum of lumps and bruises.

However, when I entered college, I was required to take the
College Entrance Examination. Later in the day, with an expression of shock and anguish, the school psychologist pulled me

aside and said that he had never seen a lower score in twenty years of experience. He seriously entertained the question as to whether I was really alive, and predicted that I would never survive the semester. "What is a semester?" I asked.

But what did he know of the power of Hermes?

> Did he know that sports had propelled me from the open-hearth, the blast furnace, and the soaking-pits of the steel mills into a world of boundless choice and opportunity?

> Did he know that sports had taught me the value of co-operation, team-work, friendship, and brother-hood — which no book, or lecture, or essay could possibly convey?

> Did he know that sports had provided me with poise, confidence, patience, discipline — and that I fully appreciated the subtle relationship between the body and the mind?

No — he didn't — for the academicians are much like the clergy. They like to pigeon-hole information; they want to simplify experience; they desire to eliminate contradictions; they work to break everything down to a single category. Thus, to the professors, a "jock" is a mindless person and athletics are beneath their highbrow manner. (Little do they know that in ancient Egypt Hermes was also the God of learning.)

Obviously, there are evils and excesses in all religions — and the glorification of athletics is no exception. It is never free of corruption. There are pitfalls and false prophets.

> The Monistic Philosophers of sports would have us believe that it is the solution to everything. With the zeal of the revivalist, we are told that it is good for the heart, for impotence, for delinquency, for popularity, for foreign relations, and even as a substitute for war. Such a view produces a variety of health-nuts, sports-freaks, and crazed joggers — who while seeking salvation, find nothing but athlete's feet. I have never liked the zealots of sports.

> The Commercial Hucksters of sports would have us believe that it is crucial to the economy. With the tongue of the serpent, we are told that it supports colleges, increases the revenue of cities, attracts television advertising, and contributes to the vitality of the capitalist system. Such

a view produces athletes who are pampered, corrupt, overpaid — who while losing their original purity, succumb to the sins of pride and avarice. I have never liked the prostitutes of sports.

The Sexist Apologists of sports would have us believe that it is a male dominion. With the logic of oppression, we are told that it demands a strength, courage, and aggressiveness which is absent in women — and that they are more properly positioned as cheerleaders, spectators, and camp-followers. Such a view produces a society of competitive men and passive women — who, while shaking their pom-poms, are chillingly denied their full potential. I have never liked the machos of sports.

The Violent Aborigines of sports would have us believe that it is an emotional release. With the wisdom of Psychology 101, we are told that it creates an escape valve for anti-social behavior; that it satisfies the blood-lust of the human animal; and that it ultimately protects our children from the rapists and muggers who are quietly enjoying a TV hockey game. Such a view produces a person who, while posing as an athlete, is given the license to kill. I have never liked the ghouls of sports.

In short, I would like to disassociate myself from those who distort the function of Hermes. He is not the God of the Universe; he is not the God of Capitalism; he is not the God of Sexism; and he is not the God of Riots and Bloodshed. They are other gods, and should not be confused with the son of Zeus and Maia.

Nor is Hermes the God of conventional religion, who trafficks in magic and superstition. A sneak and a rascal, he never appears when you call him.

I remember when our college team was in the finals for the National Championship. Our coach was obsessed with the need to win. In the locker room, he said in a hoarse whisper, "OK, you guys, this is the BIG one. Let's all say the Lord's Prayer — for luck!"

So, we all knelt down on the cold floor, in a circle, huddled together at the feet of our coach, and reverently bowed our heads. Nothing but silence for several minutes . . .

Finally, the coach said: "OK, you guys, who wants to give the first line." Again, nothing but silence . . . until the coach realized that no one knew the Lord's Prayer — not even himself!

Eventually, as I recall, someone led us in "Now I Lay Me Down to Sleep" — but it did nothing for our game — and we lost.

But if Hermes is not a conventional God, he is no less real to those who seek him. For I have seen the result of his awesome power; and I have been recipient of his amazing grace; and I have witnessed the special quality of his profound revelation. He does exist!

First, he reveals a healthy and primitive humanism, which our civilization has largely forgotten with its emphasis on material objects.

> Those who would attack the potential of the human species have never really seen the coordinated strength of a Hank Aaron; or the smooth flow of a Dorothy Hamill; or the cat-like moves of a Muhammad Ali; or the controlled contortions of a Rick Barry; or the unending rhythm of a Gene Washington; or the mental concentration of a Jack Nicklaus; or the hidden power of a Chris Evert.

What a marvelous instrument! What a priceless treasure! What a beautiful form! Like Atlas and Hercules, it is truly made to carry the burdens of the world.

Second, he reveals the boundaries and limitations of human achievement, which our civilization has largely ignored with its emphasis on inevitable progress.

> Those who would worship themselves as Gods have never really known the humiliation of defeat; or the collision of disaster; or the fall on the slope; or the pain in the night; or the count of the referee; or the lungs crying for air; or the foot slipping with the starter's gun; or the mind failing to control the fingers; or the crack of a bone on a hardwood floor; or grown men crying together.

What a sensitive instrument! What a delicate treasure! What a brittle form! Like Hector and Achilles, it is truly made to be broken and to die.

Third, he reveals the courage and nobility of the human creature, which our civilization has largely neglected with its emphasis on despair and cynicism.

> Those who would surrender all hope for the future have never really noticed the discipline of a swimmer; or the sacrifice of a weight-lifter; or the solidarity of a soccer team; or the dream of a pole vaulter; or the fury of a

>sprinter; or the faith of a mountain climber; or the
>intelligence of a yachtsman; or the ceaseless struggle
>of a rookie anything.

What a nimble instrument! What a sturdy treasure! What a
persistent form! Like Sisyphus and Ulysses, it is truly made
to be stubborn and to persevere.

Finally, I think it is Hermes who reveals a power beyond
the ordinary experience, which our civilization has largely
repudiated with its emphasis on secularity.

I remember one of the final games of my Senior year in
college:

>I had not practiced any differently, or eaten any differ-
>ently, or rested any differently — yet everything was
>certainly different! Like nothing before! It is best
>compared to a wonderful dream of floating through
>space — as my speed was increased, my reactions
>were automatic, my mind and body were in perfect
>communication, and every time I shot the ball
>(often not looking) it split the cords with uncanny
>accuracy.

While I broke the record that day, with 39 points and 22 rebounds,
I could never accept it as a personal achievement. For I knew
there was something beyond my own capacity; some mysterious
energy, some infinite power, some awesome source of creativity
which I could barely comprehend — and which seemed to be
WHOLLY OTHER.

It was an experience that would later lead to a renewed
interest in religion; to the joining of a church; to the profession
of the ministry; and to the conviction that God exists in everything — if God could exist in a third-rate "jock" from Western
Pennsylvania.

So, thank you, Hermes — for that brief glimpse.

>*May you continue to touch the imagination*
>   *of other boys and girls, strengthening their bodies*
>   *and giving them dreams.*
>*May you continue to sit on the shoulders of other men*
>   *and women, teaching them discipline*
>   *and extending their grasp.*

May you continue to exist on the streets,
    on the playgrounds, and on all the fields
    of the world – as they, too, are the highways
    of ambition, the halls of learning,
    and the churches of God.

For now and forever more – AMEN!

Chapter II

To Do Justice and To Love Kindness

"Each of us is an artist
Whose task it is to shape life
Into some semblance of the pattern
He dreams about.
So let us be about our task.
The materials are very precious —
and perishable."
— ARTHUR GRAHAM

A View From the Dump

It was twenty-five years ago — but I still remember!

I watched the perpetually burning materials as they contributed their pungent smells and choking vapors to the murky sky above the field. Amidst the tended flames of the Inferno, I had the insubstantial feeling that must exist on the borders of Hell, where everything, wavering among heat waves, is transported to another dimension. I could imagine ragged and distorted souls picked over by scavengers for what might usefully survive.

Yet I was not the scholarly Dante, viewing the fires of Purgatory in search of the meaning of life and death. For his was a journey into the world of imagination, while mine was a journey into the world of reality. I was a fifteen year old garbageman in hip boots, forking over the rubbish in the county dump for nineteen dollars a week. The only scavengers were flies, and rats, and pigeons.

It was Noah Webster who defined garbage as "Any worthless, offensive, or inferior matter," and there on the county dump lay the shabby debris of life:

> The waxen fragment of an old record that had stolen a human heart;

> The wilted flowers among crushed beer cans and broken bottles;

> The glass eye of a baby doll that had opened and closed on Christmas morning;

> And the old sandwich wrappings, the castaway knife, a twisted spoon, the skeleton of a fish, and the bed I had slept on as a child.

Fork it over. Give it air. Watch it burn. Fork it over again. It was all a maze of disconnected, floating meanings — and would be, until the last person perished.

Loren Eiseley understood. If the archaeologist is awake to memories of the dead cultures sleeping around us, to their destiny, and to the nature of the universe they inhabited — then the garbageman is the last grubber among things of our own civilization, both our grocery bills and the hymns to our gods.

He carries away what the people put before him; he burns what the culture no longer values; he buries what the archaeologist of the future will uncover.

In short, it is he who puts our civilization to bed — and executes the final judgment.

As a former garbageman, I am always alert to the news of my old profession, and sometimes, I must confess, I look at the news from the perspective of a dump philosopher. For example:

In Dallas: Mr. Robert Perkins was brought to trial for assaulting Mrs. Sandra Perkins with a can of soup, after she repeatedly refused to carry out the trash. I noticed that it was Campbell's Tomato Soup.

In Washington: The FBI borrowed a garbage truck and uniforms from the Sanitation Department and stole a coding machine from the Czech Embassy while in disguise. I noticed that they forgot to empty the garbage.

In New York: A wildcat walkout by the Sanitation Union turned Fun City into Stink City, with 28,000 tons of refuse piling up each day on the streets. I noticed that the opponents of the pay increase did not help out in the emergency.

In Georgetown: A reporter took five bags of garbage from the home of Henry Kissinger in order to do a garbology profile of the Secretary of State. I noticed that when Mr. Kissinger reported he was revolted by the action — the garbage was returned to his doorstep.

But the big news about garbage is still the sheer volume of material cast away by the dirtiest of all animals.

Garbage killing the lakes and streams —
Garbage covering the deserts and mountains —
Garbage floating in the silence of space —
Garbage found in the stomach of a shark —
Garbage in our eyes, and ears, and fingertips.

And occasionally, out of the human need to dissolve, to demolish, to destroy: the limp body of a bird, or the still form of a pet, or the gray tissue of a human fetus appears on the dump. It is a grim testimony to our powers of dissolution.

I once worked with a man who had spent over 25 years in the dump. He was a gnarled old professional, with deceptively muscled arms, a curvature of the spine, and a cigarette that appeared to be sculpted to his mouth. While he seldom spoke to the younger workers, he would often relieve them of the more difficult tasks — by emptying the heaviest cans, working next to the hottest flames, and forking the dangerous plastic materials. It was he who first demonstrated to me how spray cans explode!

One day, while working near the old man, I observed him reaching down into the garbage. He picked up a battered vase, held it up to the light, rolled it between his fingers, and then placed it carefully on the ground. In the next instant, he dug a small hole with his fork, into which he put the vase, and covered it with earth. When he was finished (and it only took a minute) he patted the mound gently — like the ritual at a grave.

What was the meaning of the ceremony?

Perhaps he realized that here was a once beautiful object, wrenched from deep veins of rock, boiled in a great crucible, and carried miles from its origin. It had been defined before its existence, named and given shape in the puff of air we call a word. And that word had been evoked in the profound darkness of a living brain which, with all its contained powers and lurking paradoxes, had arisen in ways we can never trace.

Should it be destroyed with a push of the fork? Should it be cast back into the fire? Or should this forlorn object be gently laid to rest in a proper tomb — with respect and solemnity?

The old man decided, and it was saved. I can well imagine the puzzled expression of the archaeologist of the future as he discovers a Woolworth vase.

Of course, no one listens to the musings of a dump philosopher.

> Most people in our world never have seen the local dump. They are embarrassed by their own drippings.

> Most people in our society have assigned the garbage-man to the bottom of the social scale. They fare no better in the communist countries.

> And most people in the ecological movement live in Palo Alto, Grosse Point, and White Plains. They are experts in abstraction.

"After all, they seem to be saying, "what does a garbageman know about garbage?"

I read an editorial the other day, written by a leading advocate of ecology. He said in part:

> "We discover that we humans are linked in an all-embracing web from the one-celled algae to the magnificent redwood. Everything inter-relates, we are not apart, we are inseparable and indivisible with the universe. Our salvation lies in our relationship with all life forms. Our worship is inspired by the ineffable beauty of mountains, oceans, seashores, wilderness, the sky, and in the regularity of seasons and cycles. As Blake once expressed it:
>
> > 'To see a world in a grain of sand
> > and a heaven in a wild flower.' "

It is a wonderful collection of words and sentiments — but I find it a little disagreeable.

I have no argument with the view that we should always value the good and the beautiful, but I do have an argument with the view that we should *only* value the good and the beautiful. It is, I think, a significant mistake of the ecological movement, which is somewhat removed from the reality of the world.

> If we are linked in an all-embracing web with everything, then we should be linked with the candy wrapper and the popsicle stick.
>
> If our salvation lies in our relationship with all life forms, then it should lie in our relationship with the fetus and the chicken bone.
>
> If our worship is inspired by the beauty of mountains, ocean, sky, and wilderness, then it should be inspired by the reality of compost, toilets, dumps and garbage cans.
>
> And if we are really concerned with the regularity of the seasons and cycles, then we should be concerned with the process of dissolution, and decay, and death.

In other words, why should we selectively ignore the grossly physical?

Indeed, perhaps even Blake should be corrected with the insights of another poet:

> "The pride of wrights, the joy of smiths abide
> In fallen things –
> In tattered carpetings,
> In blackamoors and chamber pots.
> Useless, they stay there in their show of pride
> Under the naked watts.

Is that not childhood in the corner there,
Color and riot
So dark now, and so quiet?
To linger there would be unwise.
What if the tongues of wagons beat the air,
And dolls opened their eyes?
The shoe forsaken is essential last.
The cobbler fled
Barefooted with the dead;
His cunning stayed upon the soul.
Poor boot, your consolation is your past —
Now broken, you are whole.
Ah, this is the imperium of things,
Things in themselves
These crammed and dusty shelves
Contain in us the things we wrought.
These bronze, unbarbered heads are not our kinds
But subjects of our thought."

I wonder: is anything really worthless? Should we not be sensitive to the dying emanations from objects that bespeak our humanity — even those we most deny?

When William Butler Yeats was in the autumn of his life, he asked his secretary to go through his poetry and point out all the abstract words he could find. The number was so startling that Yeats embarked upon a systematic attempt to de-emphasize abstraction in his work. For he was convinced that a vague romantic language was the curse of the poetry of his time, and that all poetry must be more strongly rooted in the actual and physical.

Why?

I think he realized that romantic notions and visionary goals, not attached to the sweat and blood of the real world, are bound to fail.

I think he realized that all existing things, however low, or mean, or odd, have a unique value in themselves, or can be used for other purposes.

And I think he realized, too, that everything: the burning materials, the pungent smells, the choking vapors, and the human attendant — are all vitally linked together.

So it is an aging Irish poet who best expresses the thoughts of a young garbageman knee-deep in the shabby debris of life, forking it over, giving it air, watching it burn, and forking it over again. He writes:

> "Those masterful images because complete
> Grew in pure mind, but out of what began?
> A mound of refuse or the sweepings of a street
> Old kettles, old bottles, and a broken can,
> Old iron, old bones, old rags, that raving slut
> Who keeps the till. Now that my ladders gone,
> I must lie down where all the ladders start,
> In the foul rag-and-bone shop of the heart."

Perhaps we will only keep the world clean, when we see all litter as a part of ourselves; and perhaps we will only know salvation, when we see ourselves as a part of litter.

At least that is the view from the dump.

A Fugitive in My Attic

I challenged the law of the government of the United States of America! Doctor Spock, Huey Newton, Martin Luther King, Lieutenant Calley, Father Berrigan, Charles Manson — and me! I have been a part of that mixture of various kinds of madness, national frustration, and degrees of guilt and innocence which not even Solomon would comprehend. I am neither proud nor ashamed.

It all began in July of 1968. A young man knocked on the door of my church office in Watertown, Massachusetts. The stranger was visibly nervous and mentally confused. He was dressed in soiled slacks and torn tee-shirt, and with unshaven face, long tousled hair and darting eyes, he reminded me of a character from Dostoyevsky — from *Crime and Punishment* or *The Possessed.*

In a lengthy monologue, punctuated by sobs, at times losing the sequence of his story and lapsing into silence, he pieced together an outline of his shattered life. Little did I know at the time how it would affect my own.

Jim Smith was nineteen years of age — born in a small town in northern California. He was the oldest of six children and a high school graduate. His father was a veteran of World War II, permanently disabled and living on a government pension. Unable to support his growing family (and proud of his own achievements in the military) he encouraged his eldest son to pursue a military career.

Of course, Jim could not have avoided the decision in any event — since he had no interest in higher education and fully expected to be caught in the draft. So at the age of eighteen, he enlisted in the Marine Corps and was sent to a training camp in southern California.

43

The young recruit did not adjust well to the military life. It was the first time he had been separated from home and family. He was afraid, petulant, and immature. The normal hazing routine of the camp only increased his anxieties, causing him to hate his superiors and to withdraw into himself. On the first weekend leave Jim almost decided to go AWOL, but finally ruled against it.

A few months later, Jim Smith was transferred to the East coast. Unlike the great majority of recruits who somehow survive the rigors of basic training and succeed in adjusting to the routine of military discipline, Jim brought his troubles with him. He disobeyed an officer — and he insulted an officer.

A confinement in the stockade did not improve his attitude.

A visit to the psychiatrist did not result in peace of mind.

A meeting with the chaplain did not result in peace of soul. The despair, the desperation, the anxiety, only seemed to increase as the days wore on.

The military career of Jim Smith ended just five months after the enlistment. He went over the hill on a weekend pass. An aimless flight through many states, over many thousands of miles, finally brought him to my door in Watertown — tired, depressed, and utterly confused.

It was quite by accident. He had no friends in the area. The police were suspicious of him. He had not eaten in several days. Yet it was not the typical fugitive I met that day (if any are typical), but a desperate adolescent-man who wanted nothing more than to be left alone. The church was an island of rest.

I listened to the story. I knew long before he concluded that there could be no pleasant solution to the problem, but I questioned him closely.

I said: "Do you have any injuries or ailments that might lead to a physical disability?" . ... . "No, the doctors examined me recently."

I said: "What did the psychiatrist say about your mental condition? Did he mention a psychiatric discharge?" . . . "No, he said I was normal."

I said: "Is it possible that you could apply for a hardship deferment in order to support your family?" . . . "I don't think so. My father won't speak to me."

I said: "Then what about a CO status? Would you say that you are morally opposed to serving in the military and to committing acts of violence?"... "I don't know what you mean."

"How do you feel right now?"... "I'm frightened!"

It was obviously no time for profound observations.

So I escorted Jim to a restaurant where he enjoyed an ample meal. I found him some clothes and brought him home to the parsonage for a good night's sleep. In the morning, we shared breakfast together and discussed the future.

In reality, there were only two major alternatives. The first was to leave the country. It was a relatively easy undertaking with little risk and certain freedom. But I warned him that it would mean an almost total break with family and friends — and perhaps a lifetime of exile.

The second alternative was to voluntarily surrender. In the short run this was the less appealing choice, in view of the severe penalties then being meted out by military courts. But in the long run surrender would probably result in a shorter sentence and more certain return to civilian life in the United States. Between exile and prison — only Jim could decide.

I harbored the fugitive for three days and three nights. It was the time he needed to rest, to sort out his thoughts, and to plan for the future. At no time did I condone his action. I did not recommend a particular alternative. I merely tried to support him as a person — to provide a trusting environment without tension and fear.

In time, he began to relax. He played with my children. He joked about his brothers and sisters. He began to laugh again. I liked him very much.

And then, I remember, one sunny morning at the door of the church, we shook hands and murmured our goodbyes. He disappeared. God only knows his destination, and whether he reached it ... safely. I never saw him again.

Yet, I will never forget him. For Jim Smith was only the first of over three hundred fugitives I have known. He was the original impetus for the founding of an organization dedicated to helping those young men who were refugees from the military system. Thus, my life was changed.

I organized a select group of Unitarian and Quaker families in New England as an Underground Railroad. I provided counseling, food, clothing, and shelter — much like the sanctuary of the Medieval Church. I named the organization *Parents Opposed to the War* (POW), because I thought all parents should be concerned with all children, and because I believed there were many kinds of POW's in our society.

I met all kinds in the next four years!

Jim Smith the Loser. He had applied for a CO status in a conservative industrial city in New England. But the Draft Board only accepted about ten per cent of the CO applications — usually those of the sons of prominent individuals in the community. It was the quota system. He fled to Canada.

Jim Smith the Immigrant. He was a recent arrival from Portugal. He applied for a CO status, but could not defend his position at the hearing of the Selective Service Board. He spoke only broken English and did not have a lawyer. He fled to Canada.

Jim Smith the Homosexual. He had enlisted in the Army, only to be harassed and beaten by the other soldiers. He was offered a psychiatric discharge, but he did not happen to believe that homosexuality was a psychiatric problem. He fled to Canada.

Jim Smith the Activist. He was opposed to war, the military, the government, uniforms, the draft board, and filling out forms. He organized resistance rallies and distributed literature at induction centers. He lived in the Underground.

Jim Smith the Coward. He deeply feared the military for reasons known only to himself. When he received his notice of induction, he purposely staged a felony which led to his arrest. He went to prison.

Jim Smith the Black. He had merely visited the Selective Service Office to pick up some forms. A racial slur from a secretary led to a personal rage that virtually destroyed the office. He fled to the Underground. He later surrendered.

Jim Smith the Son. He had lived with his mother, who was paralyzed from the waist down. His work as a fisherman was the only source of income for a family of four. His hardship deferment was denied. The appeal was denied. He and the family moved to Canada.

Jim Smith the Cripple. He had been declared unfit for military service by two independent doctors. He had

had two operations on his knee and a third scheduled. He passed the Army exam. He hobbled off to Canada.

These are the human beings involved in the continuing dispute over amnesty. They are not statistical abstractions — not all saints and heroes — and not all weaklings and malcontents. Should we welcome them home with music, and parades, and medals of honor? Should we welcome them home with trials, and hearings, and conditional amnesty? No. We should simply welcome them home.

And why did I challenge the law of the United States of America by harboring fugitives in a time of war? I suppose there were many reasons.

It was never moral certitude! It would be comforting to think that my own moral judgment is superior to the law of the land — but I have too much respect for the rule of law and too little for my own wisdom. Breaking the law is a dangerous precedent. Moral courage is often recklessness. Defiance can be another word for vanity. So I had many sleepless nights.

Yet I kept meeting new Jim Smiths:

> The young deserter, who suddenly froze when asked to fire a weapon;
> The young Harvard student, who had read the manuscript of the Pentagon Papers;
> The young farmer, who wanted only to work the soil of his native land —

Plus those who had lost to the quota system in their small home towns; those who had no power to cheat the draft; those who had suffered prejudice from race, religion, or education; those who had fearful premonitions of the unknown; and those who had lost all faith in the future. I had to help them.

I was reminded of the Unitarians and Quakers of over a hundred years ago. They were not arrogant — but humble. They were not radicals — but progressives. They were not traitors — but patriots. Yet they had organized an Underground Railroad: opposing the laws of Congress, defying the authority of the state, and risking their lives in defense of fugitives from slavery.

I realized that my spiritual ancestors, though reluctant to break their oath of allegiance to flag and country, had given expression to a responsibility of another kind — on another level.

> It is the responsibility to protect the weak and the oppressed.

It is the responsibility to cry out against the abuse of power.

It is the responsibility of each and every person for the pain of every other person.

In short, it is the moral imperative, the demand of conscience, the ethical commitment — which no state can control and no law silence.

I concluded, therefore, that I was forced to enter into a conspiracy of love against the government of the United States. It was a conspiracy to aid and defend the new slaves of our society.

Slaves through the accident of their births;

Slaves through the madness and hysteria of war;

Slaves through the inconsistency of laws;

Slaves through the need for anger and revenge.

Without arrogance or fear, I decided to help them — and I am neither proud nor ashamed.

A few weeks ago, I was leading a workshop at a church conference in Ithaca, New York. When the session was over, a husky young man approached the lectern and introduced himself. He said:

"I'm sure you don't recognize me, Reverend Rankin, but eight years ago, when I was AWOL from the Army, you helped to straighten things out. I just want to thank you and tell you I'm now studying for the Unitarian-Universalist ministry."

And to tell you the truth, it brought tears to my eyes — as all the Jim Smiths appeared in my mind and filled my heart. I stumbled away.

"Where do I get my passion for justice
which torments me and irritates me and
makes me angry? I cannot account for it.
It is my God, my religion, my all!"
— PROUDHON

Confessions of an Anarchist Clergyman

The word, "Anarchist," unsettles most people in the Western world. It suggests disorder, violence, uncertainty. We have good reason for fearing those conditions, because we have been living with them for a long time, not in anarchist societies (there have never been any), but in exactly those societies most fearful of anarchy — the powerful nation states of modern times.

Anarchos, the original Greek word, means "without a ruler," and has been used in a general context to mean either the negative condition of unruliness, or the positive condition of being unruled because rule is unnecessary. In modern times:

> The anarchists conceive a society in which all the mutual relations of its members are regulated, not by laws, not by authorities, whether self-imposed or elected, but by mutual agreements between the members of that society in accordance with the ever-growing requirements of a free life.

It is a philosophy of radical democracy, extreme individualism, and mutual responsibility.

Of course, the only purpose of any philosophy is to have an orderly system of ideals by which to live and to interpret the world. Ortega y Gassett put it simply:

> *We cannot live on the human level without ideals.*
> *Upon them depends what we do. Living is nothing more*
> *or less than doing one thing instead of another.*

In other words, the way in which we experience and interpret the world depends on the kinds of ideals that fill our minds. If they are mainly small, weak, superficial, and incoherent — life

49

will appear insipid, uninteresting, petty, and chaotic. If they are mainly large, strong, deep, and intelligible — life will appear rich, exciting, significant, and ordered. It is all in what we choose.

In the realm of political philosophy, I have chosen anarchism — not to be shocking, or dramatic, or different — but merely to clarify the meaning of my own existence. Unknown to many, I have been an anarchist for twenty years, which is considerably longer than I have been a theist, a minister, or a Unitarian-Universalist.

> As a child, I observed the frightful effects of a large corporation as it depersonalized, oppressed, and plundered a working-class community.
>
> As a college freshman, I drank deeply from the springs of criticism and gentleness as created by Zeno, Lao-tzu, and Jesus; by Thoreau, Tolstoy, and Shelley.
>
> As a graduate student, I was elected to serve on the Board of the Anarchist Association of America, the only organized group in the Western Hemisphere.
>
> As a Professor of Political Science, I was the author of a monthly article on anarchism which was published in a leading American magazine.

I have not changed my views since entering the ministry. In my opinion (which has no official standing in the church) anarchism is the only political theory that combines an essentially revolutionary attitude with a philosophy of freedom. In my opinion (which has sometimes led to personal and professional grief) anarchism is the only militant libertarian doctrine left in the world today. I have not changed my views at all.

But I have already presented the issue with more bravado than I honestly wished to convey. Actually, I have always found it difficult to follow the philosophy I have chosen. Like most people, I am not always wise enough, or strong enough, or consistent enough in the pursuit of my own ideals. In the end, I know that I am only a human being, who achieves an existence which is something below ultimate perfection and heroic proportion, and something above meaningless tragedy and inward disgrace.

I must confess, for example, that I am often influenced by popular opinion. To most, anarchy is malign chaos. The stereotype of the anarchist as a cold-blooded assassin who attacks with dagger or bomb the pillars of established society has been perpetrated by governments which came into being through violence, which maintain themselves in power through violence, and which use violence constantly to destroy other nations.

In contrast, the anarchists have always argued that a revolution cannot be achieved by force of arms. The real revolution is prepared in the minds and behavior of people, not as an act, but as a process.

> It means starting this moment to do away with authoritarian, cruel relationships between men and women, between parents and children, between one kind of worker and another. It takes place in everyday life, in families, on streets, in neighborhoods, in places of work. It is a revolution of the whole being and the whole culture, not the senseless bombing of a supermarket, or the savage killing of innocent people — in the manner of the organized state.

Yet the equation of anarchism with nihilism and terrorism remains deep in the popular mind, and I am often tempted to abandon my ideals.

I must confess, for example, that I am often depressed by the current direction of society. Are we moving toward centralization, concentration, depersonalization; or are we moving toward individualism, independence, and freedom? There can be no possible doubt as to which direction is the more desirable; but I am afraid that at the moment, everywhere in the world, we are moving in the wrong direction.

In contrast, the anarchists have always seen progress, not in terms of a steady increase in material wealth and complexity of living, but rather in terms of the moralizing of society by the abolition of authority, inequality, and economic exploitation.

> Bigness is the nemesis of anarchism, whether the bigness is that of public or private bureaucracies, corporations or unions, churches or pentagons — because from bigness comes impersonality, insensitivity, and a lust for power. Hence the title of a popular book, *Small is Beautiful*, which means that small is freer, more creative, enjoyable, enduring — for such is the anarchist faith.

Yet the chaotic growth of our cities; the inscrutable complexity of our governments; the factory environment of our schools; and the voracious appetite of our economic giants are all in the opposite direction, and I am often tempted to abandon my ideals.

I must confess, for example, that I am often discouraged by the massive flight from freedom. In the past, it took the form of accepting the promises of politicians, or the communism of Marx, or the quest for the fountain of youth. But today it is presented in the more subtle forms of personality transplants, or fascist religions, or media gurus in folded bedsheets. For the mind has the urge to simplify; and the body has the urge to rest; and the senses have the urge to flee the razor's edge. Is there not somewhere an island, a potion, a utopia — if only for a moment?

In contrast, the anarchists have always focused on the larger question of human society, on the social roots of alienation.

> When Jesus assailed the establishment, he was not interested in escaping pain, but in changing the structure of society.
>
> When Tolstoy attacked the institution of slavery, he was not interested in personal popularity, but in the freedom of all people.
>
> When Thoreau rejected the centralized state, he was not interested in singular salvation, but in universal peace and justice.
>
> And when Bakunin said: "I detest communism, because it is the negation of liberty and because I can conceive nothing human without liberty," he was not interested in the leading guru of his time, but in the liberation of the human spirit.

Yet the flight from freedom is epidemic today, and I am often tempted to abandon my ideals.

There are so many temptations! Dare I list them? Ease — luxury — frivolity — self-pity — acclaim — security — success — the list is almost endless, as I think back on a life not always consistent with the ideals of philosophy.

> "Our bitterest wine," says the poet, is always
> drained from crushed ideals."

Yet, I do not believe that I have completely abandoned them.

> "For ideals are like stars; you will not succeed
> in touching them. But like the sea-faring man
> on the desert of waters, you choose them
> as your guides, and following them,
> you reach your destiny."

If I have strayed from time to time — I have not altered course.

I have been influenced by popular opinion, but I continue to believe in the need to resist all forms of coercion and control. So I shall endeavor to live as an individual, to develop freely, and if necessary to be isolated in a prison rather than submit to the indignities of any power or system.

I have been depressed by the current direction of society, but I continue to believe in the need to pose a counter-ideal. So I shall endeavor to help in the urgent task of survival, until the movement for centralization loses its impetus like all historical movements, and the moral forces that depend on individual choice and judgment can reassert themselves in the midst of its corruption.

I have been discouraged by the massive flight from freedom, but I continue to believe in the need to stand on our own moral feet. So I shall endeavor to become aware of justice as an inner fire, and to learn that the still, small voice of my own heart speaks more truly than all the choruses of propaganda that daily assault my outer ears.

> "Look into the depths of your own beings," said the doomed anarchist. "Seek out the truth and realize it yourselves. You will find it nowhere else."

With all my weaknesses and failings — I continue to believe!

It was fifteen years ago that I put a prayer in my wallet. I had received it from an elderly statesman of American anarchism who, for most of his life, had operated a soup-kitchen for the poor and destitute in Denver, Colorado. It is a good reminder of my own ideals:

> *"I must learn to think differently before the revolution can come. That alone can bring the revolution.*
>
> *If my object is to secure liberty, I must learn to do without authority and compulsion.*
>
> *If I intend to live in peace and harmony with my brothers and sisters, I must learn to cultivate a respect for all.*
>
> *If I want to work together with them for a mutual growth, I must learn to practice a mutual cooperation.*
>
> *For the revolution means more than the changing of institutions.*
>
> *It means the establishment of new values and relationships.*

It means a changed attitude of person to person, beginning with myself.

It means a different spirit in individual and collective life.

And it is a spirit that cannot be born overnight. It is a spirit to be cultivated, to be nurtured and reared, as the most delicate flower is, for indeed it is the flower of a beautiful existence.

Be patient. Be strong. Be loving."

AMEN!

"God may be the chaos —
Missed in our neatness and order —
Who shuns the glistening temple
To walk in the gray repositories
Of twisted and divided souls."
— EDWARD FROST

We Are Cain's Children

It was a clear, sunny day.

I was playing basketball with my two sons at the local junior high school. Across the playground, about fifty yards away, I saw a fist fight develop between two young men. Two other men were watching the action and cheering for one of the fighters.

As I began to walk toward the battle, I could see that the popular fighter was losing badly. A hard punch to the nose brought blood to his face and he tried to wipe it with his sleeve. Suddenly, the two bystanders jumped the other young man, knocking him to the ground, pounding him with their fists, and kicking his head into the cement.

When I arrived, he was bleeding heavily from the head and face, screaming like a trapped animal, and pleading for his life. But they continued to kick and punch (all three), uninfluenced by pity or mercy, until I pushed one of the men and told him to stop. It was then that they turned on me, and I stared into the eyes of absolute hatred, and I sensed the brutal urge to destroy, and I knew I had entered a primitive world of raw and naked violence.

It was not the first experience.

As a child in a tough steel mill city, I had learned the lessons of the street, where violence lurks in every stranger, every shadow, every form.

As a fighter in the ring, I had learned the lessons of sport, where violence is disguised as play, as business, as healthy entertainment.

As a minister in the church, I had learned the lessons of counseling, where violence is neatly dressed over knife, or gun, or a brittle snap of the mind.

Yet, I have never gotten used to violence. It is still so mysterious, so powerful, so terrifying, that I sometimes feel it is the other side of God!

Today, violence is a frequent companion in San Francisco. Incongruous, perhaps, in the beautiful city of St. Francis of Assisi, it is nonetheless both menacing and deadly.

In our schools, my son is threatened with an ice-pick in the fourth grade; my daughter is victimized by gangs at recess; and my other son is frightened and abused at almost every hour.

In our church, my parishioners are mugged on the sidewalk; their cars are stripped or stolen on Sunday mornings; and many will not even approach the church when the sun goes down.

In our neighborhoods, my friends are robbed at gunpoint; their homes and apartments are looted at all hours of the day and night; and some have experienced the vicious crime of rape.

Indeed, it is difficult to read the words of St. Francis: "Where hate rules, let us bring love; where sorrow, joy" — in a city with armed guards on the buses and streetcars, iron bars on the doors and windows, police dogs in the parks and basements, and a loaded revolver in the drawer by the bed.

Not too long ago, it was believed that violence could be eliminated from the world. Remember those wonderful predictions?

The Generals said: "The war to end all wars in Europe will usher in a thousand years of peace."

The Educators said: "The proper rearing of children will produce a loving and compassionate people."

The Scientists said: "The application of technology will ultimately destroy the causes of violence."

The Politicians said: "The founding of the United Nations will be the beginning of a world community."

How naive! How ignorant! How mistaken! For violence is a foe that can never be defeated. It is an enemy within the lines.

In the cartoon *Peanuts*, little Linus is looking at his hands and speaking to Lucy:

"Hands are fascinating things. I like my hands. I think I have nice hands. My hands seem to have a lot of character. These are hands which may accomplish marvelous works. They may build mighty bridges, or heal the sick,

or hit home runs, or write stirring novels. These are
hands which may someday change the course of
history."

And Lucy, who has patiently listened, says simply:

"They've got jelly on them!"

From the attempts of Pontius Pilate and Lady Macbeth to
cleanse their hands, to more modern drama, dirty hands have
been used as an outward sign of an inner disgrace. She is really
saying to Linus:

"There is more to your hands than you are willing to
admit. They can build or DESTROY. They can heal or
HURT. They can love or HATE. Why are you blind to
the violence in yourself? What is this masquerade?"

And poor Linus! He has been taught to believe that children
are innocent creatures; that human beings are basically good;
and that violence and aggression are due only to certain problems
in the social structure which have nothing to do with him.

When one hundred civilians were slaughtered at My-Lai,
it was a Linus general who called it: "A breakdown
in the system of command."

When the National Guard shot students at a major
university, it was a Linus jury who called it: "A
mistake in judgment."

When a man was knifed in the back in the city, it was a
Linus sociologist who called it: "An act of personal
alienation."

And when I was attacked and robbed in Dorchester,
Massachusetts, it was a Linus policeman who called
it: "A problem of not having streetlights."

Poor Linus! Not only is HE not to blame, but he creates a lie to
cover the reality. "Whose death? Whose son? Whose brother?
There must be some mistake! It has nothing to do with me!"

Is it so difficult to admit the truth? Must we always resort
to lies, evasions, duplicities? Is it always "those other people" —
so different than ourselves? Consider three basic facts:

1. Violence is a perennial ingredient in history, as
common as clothes, shelter, and eating — with no
evidence to indicate that it will ever be eliminated.

2. Violence is deeply rooted in the human psyche, as firmly
as the cells and corpuscles of the body — with no evidence to indicate that anyone is excluded.

3. Violence is often a constructive tendency, as beneficial

and fruitful as love — with no evidence to indicate that
the species can survive without it.
Is that too difficult to admit? Are we so afraid to confront the
violence in ourselves? Must we always live with illusion?

In 1959, a fossil skull was exposed by erosion near a lake in
East Africa. It was a skull crushed into four hundred fragments
by a series of terrible blows. The being who had once animated
this skull had died on the shore. Symbolically, it was Abel.

Square-toothed, heavy-jawed, small-brained Abel! An
inoffensive creature, he lacked both the skills and the weapons
to be a hunter. In the bush, he pursued his scrounging, grubbing
existence — picking berries, munching roots, and running from
the sounds of larger animals. So innocent! So passive! Until, at
last, his skull was crushed.

Under vaster skies was Cain. More erect in posture, with
flatter feet for balance, a longer thumb for gripping, a larger brain
for storage — he killed for a living. Wandering erectly through
the forests and the plains with his crudely fashioned weapons,
and cursed in so many ways, he always, always, survived.

At the lake that day they met. The aggressor won and the
innocent was slain. Indeed, there should be that moment chiseled
in stone, when Cain met Abel and slew him, and wiped his bloody
weapon on the grass, and changed the course of history. For we
are the children of Cain!

In the Biblical account, Cain said to God: "My punishment
is greater than I can bear!"

> Did he know that he was a new departure in the evolution
> of the world, with the freedom and the capacity to create
> or dissolve?
> Did he then understand that the weapon in his hand was a
> blessing and a curse, with the power to reach the distant
> planets and the power to blow his own to bits?
> Did he then realize that he stood in a terrible paradox, with
> the joy of all his victories and achievements always
> threatened by the darker forces within?

Perhaps. Perhaps not. Perhaps it is for us to comprehend.

We are violent creatures — you and I. It is foolish to ignore
our inheritance by blaming it on poverty, or race, or nationalism
— for these are only the artful excuses of a thinking animal.

Again, consider:

>To satisfy our primitive eating habits, we continue to slaughter thousands of healthy animals each day, though now it is hidden from view.

>To satisfy our primitive migration pattern, we continue to challenge and kill those who cross our path, though now it is with a shiny automobile.

>To satisfy our primitive work ethic, we continue to spoil the land, pollute the streams, and waste the resources, though now it is choking the world.

>To satisfy our primitive need for play, we continue to enjoy the gory spectacle of assault and combat, though now it is a television special.

We are violent creatures — you and I. Our hands are the good, clean instruments of progress, and the dirty, jellied weapons of annihilation. It is our blessing — and our curse!

Yes — our blessing!

I am reminded of a friend named Bernie. He was a big man, about 6' 2" tall and about 230 pounds in weight. He played on the college football team with a ferociousness I had never before witnessed in a sane human being. He loved to hit, block, crush, crunch — and he liked nothing better than to knock out an opponent, break a leg, or snap a few fingers. He was affectionately known as the "Animal."

In college, we often asked ourselves: "What will ever happen to Bernie? What role could he ever possibly assume in society?" Our questions were answered a few years later when Bernie wrote to all of his old friends from the Medical School at McGill University. Today, he is a leading American surgeon — breaking bones, cutting flesh, crunching bodies — the same old Bernie!

So I wonder: Is that not the solution to our problem? Sigmund Freud once wrote:

>*We have come to see that just as the child must learn to love wisely, so he must learn to hate expeditiously: to turn destructive tendencies away from himself toward enemies that actually threaten him rather than toward the friendly and the defenseless, the more usual victims of destructive energy.*

In other words, to love and to hate, to create and to destroy, to build up and to tear down are natural tendencies of the human personality. The only difference between the energetic criminal and the energetic saint is the target toward which their energies are aimed. The instinct is exactly the same.

It is certainly more desirable, then, for a man to pound a tennis ball or walk miles in pursuit of a golf ball than to exert the same energy in attacking the skull of his neighbor or the patience of his wife. Still better, of course, would be the application of this energy to the problems of the farm, the forum, and the factory. Imagine:

A hit-man for the Mafia could be a dentist.

A pimp could be a used car salesman.

A thief could be a congressman.

A mugger could be an internal revenue agent.

A swindler could be a minister.

Certainly, the violent and aggressive spirit, properly directed, has many functions to perform. It is a matter of displacement and redirection. It is a matter of substituting socially constructive goals for the harmful goals of criminal behavior. It is a matter of channelling human aggression to create a Jesus rather than a Judas; a Pasteur rather than a Napoleon; a Martin Luther King rather than a Charles Manson. It has been done — and it can be done — if we are honest with ourselves.

Finally, to the leaders of our cities, who are concerned with the rising incidence of violence:

I recommend that you provide more play, rather than more policemen. Hands clutched to a swing replace hands clutched to a throat.

I recommend that you provide more sports, rather than more prisons. Hands shooting basketball replace hands shooting drugs.

I recommend that you provide more arts, concerts, and entertainments, rather than more guns, dogs, and vigilantes. Hands fingering a piano replace hands fingering a club.

For if the human spirit is to overcome its burden of depression, its weight of frustration, its load of anger, its mountainous supply of aggression — then it must be encouraged with the honest rewards of labor; with the delightful fruits of play; with the heightened illumination of culture; and with the investment of love and the bonds of affection which will always remain the most powerful foe of injurious violence.

Quite honestly, I must admit that I felt a little differently on the playground, when three savages were threatening to squash my head like a grapefruit. I thought to myself:

"Should I turn and walk away? No, they would continue to kick the fellow on the ground.
"Should I propose to fight them? No, they might have weapons in their jackets.
"Should I try to stall until the police arrive? No, they are miles away."

Instead, I simply leaned over the body in a professional posture; I checked under the eyelids like a seasoned doctor; I took the pulsebeat with a great show of authority; I tapped the rib-cage with a despairing shrug of the head; and I gravely announced to the silent threesome: "I think he will die!"

As they scurried off to other pastures, I walked the young man home. It did occur to me that Cain did not survive for a million years on strength alone. He is also blessed with nerve, intelligence, flexibility, a sense of humor, and a remarkable flair for deception.

In fact, I think he'll survive for a good while longer.

Chapter III
Thy Faith Hath Made Thee Whole

Confessions of a Unitarian Christian

If it is not easy to be a Unitarian, and if it is not easy to be a Christian — then it is certainly a trial to be both. I would not recommend it to a kamikaze pilot.

I remember meeting with the Pulpit Committee of a large Unitarian-Universalist church in the East. It was a very congenial meeting until one of the members asked about my personal theology. When I replied that I was a Christian, the faces turned suddenly to stone and the room went dead. Finally, after the longest meditation I had ever endured, the Chairman said: "Well, maybe we won't have to tell anyone." I said goodbye — forever!

I remember another incident, in Philadelphia, when I spoke on the theme of Christian symbolism in literature. I was asked to attend a sermon discussion after the service in the basement of the church. When I arrived, a man was screaming loudly, pounding on a table, and throwing ash-trays to the floor. As I approached, he shouted: "We have a free pulpit in this church, and we don't want any of that Christian garbage!" Like W.C. Fields, I have never returned to Philadelphia.

Finally, I remember an incident in San Francisco. Soon after I had accepted the call to be the Minister of the First Unitarian Church, I received a letter from a man who warned me to stay in Massachusetts. He was not only disturbed that I was a Christian, he was absolutely incensed over the fact that I believed in God. He warned that if I came to San Francisco my wife and children would be harmed. I wrote him a note asking him to respect my religion as much as I respected his psychosis.

I think there are many reasons why some people are angered and confused by the term, "Unitarian Christian."

First: There is the belief that since Unitarian churches are not Christian churches, you will not find Christians within them. It is a belief that does not recognize the diversity and richness of our tradition.

Second: There is the belief that since the minister should attempt to represent all church members, he should not hold to a particular theological position. It is a belief that would turn our ministers into masters of empty ceremonies.

Third: There is the belief that since Christianity is a singular theological tradition, it is impossible for the adherent to appreciate other traditions. It is a belief that does not perceive how a commitment to one object may actually heighten the awareness and appreciation of others.

Fourth: There is the belief that since Unitarianism is progressive and Christianity is reactionary, they are basically incompatible. It is a belief that is blind to the reactionary elements of Unitarianism and the progressive elements of Christianity.

Finally, there is the belief that since ministers are notoriously vague in expressing their personal opinions, it is not politically wise to be partisan in theology. It is a belief that all young ministers should consider as they dream of freedom in the pulpit. It is more difficult to be honest in theology than in any other realm.

Be prepared! I have appeared in the pulpit to speak on every conceivable topic: on defending Fidel Castro; on changing the abortion law; on impeaching the President; on amnesty for draft resisters; on the virtues of anarchism; on abolishing capital punishment; on legalizing marijuana; on supporting homosexuality; but I have never experienced the controversy caused by one simple sermon on Christianity.

> People will listen to a dry intellectual, who is
> merely quoting from the works of others;
> People will listen to an Eastern guru, who does
> not pronounce a single intelligible word;

People will listen to a chic revolutionary, who lives
in the suburbs and exists on the stock market —
but Christianity is a little too personal, a little too close, and a
little too threatening for some of our people. All tolerance is
forgotten.

It is not an unusual reaction (and I must confess — I often
enjoy the heat it engenders), for one of the most explosive questions in the entire history of civilization has been: "What is
a Christian?"

> It was a question that deeply troubled the disciples of Jesus
> while he still walked the earth. "Who is he?" "What
> does he mean?"
> It was a question that divided the leaders of the Early Church
> immediately following his death. "Who was he?" "What
> did he say?"
> It was a question that consumed the energies of a thousand
> theologians; that split the movement into a hundred
> factions; that resulted in bitterness, persecution, war,
> and inquisition.

So Unitarian-Universalists are not immune from the passion and
prejudice stimulated by the question: "What is a Christian?"

In opposition to the orthodox, I must confess that I do not
believe that Jesus was unique or creative in his theological expression. "Love God with all your heart," was the injunction of many
prophets before him. "Love your neighbor as yourself," was an
ancient commandment. "I am the son of God," was the special
dispensation enjoyed by all the Jewish people. While such expressions simplified and universalized certain elements of the
Hebrew faith, there was nothing new or novel in them.

Nor, I must confess, do I believe that Jesus was unique in
terms of his relation to the supernatural. After all, Alexander
was born of a virgin; Moses performed miracles in Egypt; Elijah
returned from the dead; and even the spirits and demons could
heal the sick. It is little wonder, that in time, Jesus refused to
perform for the crowds, "for though he had done so many miracles
before them, yet they believed not in him."

Nor, I must confess, do I believe that Jesus was unique in
his institutional ability. The Twelve Disciples were not well
organized; the Mission of the Seventy was a failure; he founded
no churches and reformed no synagogues. While the disciples
argued over the practical problems of the day, the lonely prophet

showed no concern. He left no writings, no testament, no plans for future generations.

Therefore, I do not find it helpful to define a Christian in terms of a specific theological expression, in terms of supernatural experiences, or in terms of an institutional loyalty.

> We can memorize every creed and dogma;
> We can pray for hours and hours on end;
> We can drink wine, grape-juice, or coffee;
> We can join Billy Graham, Pope Paul, or the Jesus Freaks;
> We can believe in magic, faith healing, or encounter groups.

We can do anything we like (and it might even do some good), but it is not the core of the Christian experience as I have known it.

What is a Christian?

I would identify a Christian as a person who demonstrates his love of God and the world through the example of his life. It was Jesus, himself, who said: "The works that I do in my Father's name bear witness of me. If I do not the works of my Father, believe me not. But if I do, though ye believe not me, believe the works."

So the early followers of Jesus were not interested in the abstractions of creeds and dogmas, the magic and mystery of the miracles, or even the founding of an institutional church. I think:

> They were attracted to Jesus because he represented a Supreme Model — a Supreme Model of the person who is active in the world through an ethical commitment to all human beings.
> They were attracted to Jesus because he represented the struggle between the flesh and the spirit, between rebellion and acceptance, between freedom and submission, and finally, between life and death.
> They were attracted to Jesus because he represented the stages of existence through which all people must pass: and that is why they walked in his footsteps; and that is why they shared in his suffering; and that is why they interpreted his death as their own future victory.

It was the model of his life, the style of his life, and the ultimate meaning of his life that possessed their minds, and moved their hearts, and gained their commmitment.

And what did they witness? Imagine:

> A man who called the leaders of the time a breed of vipers and told them their hearts were wicked.
> A PROTESTOR!
> A man who challenged the priests of the Temple and belittled the religious laws and customs.
> A HERETIC!
> A man who ministered to the hated Samaritans and spoke kindly to unacceptable strangers.
> A THIRD WORLDER!
> A man who ate and drank with notorious sinners and said that prostitutes would be the first in Paradise.
> A HIPSTER!
> A man who took no thought for his own reputation and comfort, but followed only the Law of Love.
> A RADICAL!
> A man who stood bravely before the judges, without whimpering, without bending, without denying the charges against him.
> A HERO!
> A man who then mounted the Cross, and while forgiving his enemies, gave himself to the mercy of God.
> A MARTYR!

These were the memories of the prophet, called Easter, which remained long after the grief of the Crucifixion. They moved Peter, the first disciple, to write: "By your good works . . . glorify God." They moved James, the brother of Jesus, to write: "Faith without works . . . is dead." In brief, that love is to be actual — love is to be incarnate — love is to be seen in our lives in the world.

> "I was hungry, and you gave me to eat;
> I was naked, and you covered me;
> I was thirsty, and you gave me to drink;
> I was sick, and you visited me;
> I was a stranger, and you took me in;
> I was in prison, and you came to me."

There is no better description of a Christian to be found in the Bible.

The perversion of the original Gospel began with the Apostle Paul, who transformed the human Jesus into the abstraction of a

Greek divinity. It was extended by the Gospel of John, written seventy years after the Crucifixion, that succeeded in making Jesus, not a model of life on earth, but an object of piety in the sky. Finally, it was sealed under the rule of the Emperor Constantine, when Christianity attained the status of an official religion. By then it was soft and tame, conservative and respectable, corrupt and perverted.

In the centuries that followed, anyone could call himself a Christian simply by announcing, "I found it!"

> They retreated to the solitude of monasteries and called themselves Christians.
> They engaged in religious wars and persecutions and called themselves Christians.
> They selfishly accumulated great fortunes and called themselves Christians.
> They gave themselves up to all manner of immorality and butchery and called themselves Christians.

For it was no longer the substance of the faith that mattered, only the form and the outward ritual.

In our own day, the oceanic risks, the daring, and the radical demands of Jesus have been squeezed down to a thin trickle of public morality.

> It is now possible to invoke his name to begin a football game.
> It is now possible to witness to Christ through a telephone conversation.
> It is now possible to be a Christian on Sunday and a bigot on Monday.

Would Jesus greet the orthodox Christians of today with a Holy Kiss? Or would he shout: "Thieves, robbers, hypocrites!"

Yet, strangely, for me at least, there is still the Easter hope and the Easter blessing. That some will call it not orthodox, I know. That some will call it not Christian, I surmise. That some will call it not Unitarian, I expect. But it is my reality.

> My reality is the Original Jesus:
> > In the swiftness of his decision, in the finality of his resolution, in the challenging and stinging hyperbole with which he tried to arouse the indolent, the dull, and the conventional — I see a person sure of himself, sure of his universe, sure of his God.

In my weakness, I need that example.

My reality is the Original Command:

> Be defined! Do something! Do something utterly real
> and radically true! No play-acting, mumbling by rote,
> posturing by precept! Commit yourself! Get the once
> and for all quality in your heart and will! To the utmost
> be true!

In my weakness, I need that advice.

My reality is the Original Gospel:

> The will of God as hunger and thirst and food and drink;
> the love of the perfect through pain and darkness and
> joy and light; the supremacy of the soul above churches
> that will cast me out; the leaving of nothing that is good
> to insignificance; the watchful eye for human suffering;
> and the courageous voice against the wrong.

In my weakness, I need that faith.

Such a faith commands and owns me.

> It makes the world fit for living —
> It gives to history a higher meaning —
> It affirms the freedom of the human spirit —
> It demands the discipline of obedience and humility —
> It requires the attributes of love and deep compassion.

For one poor soul, at least, it is a faith that exalts life and illuminates its purpose. It is my reality.

Perhaps it was Kierkegaard who best defined a Unitarian Christian (though not on purpose) when he wrote:

> *We never become a Christian — we are always*
> *in the process of becoming.*

What a marvelous mixture of openness and commitment! What a wonderful marriage of hope and faith! If it is not easy — it must be right!

Is the Reaper Really Grim?

I remember reading the great lines from Shakespeare in *Julius Caesar:*

> *Cowards die many times before their deaths;*
> *The valiant never taste of death but once.*
> *Of all the wonders that I yet have heard,*
> *It seems to me most strange that men should fear;*
> *Seeing that death, a necessary end,*
> *Will come when it will come.*

But I did not believe them.

For death was still a fearful, frightening happening, and the fear of death is a universal fear even if we think we have mastered it on many levels. I knew, for example:

> that we tend unconsciously to repress the fear and the fact of our ultimate fate because we do not wish to imagine the ending of our life on earth;

> that we resort to euphemisms, and make the dead look as if they were asleep, because we do not want to admit that they are gone forever;

> that we even have children, create monuments, and seek fame and fortune because we cannot bear the thought of our personal doom.

Our lives are poisoned by a fear of death, and much of our culture represents a response, however inadequate, to this basic fear.

I remember reading the great lines from Longfellow in *The Reaper and the Flowers:*

> *There is a reaper whose name is death,*
> *And, with his sickle keen,*
> *He reaps the bearded grain at a breath,*
> *And the flowers that grow between.*

Now that was something an ignorant coward could understand!

It was an independent old woman in my first church who began my education. She had been an active person for 101 years, and was only recently stricken with an illness that would end her life. As a novice in the ministry, I approached her room with a pocketful of prayers and tremendous anxiety. What does one say to the dying?

She was resting against two large pillows, looking out the window at the heavy New England snow. When she heard my footsteps, she turned slightly, with considerable pain in movement. Our conversation went as follows:

"Are you the new minster, or the paperboy?"

"I'm the minister."

"I could have used the paper!"

"Should I get you one?"

"No. Sit down and tell me why I should want to live."

"Thank you. I have no idea why you should want to live."

"Good! I hate advice! So now we can talk."

And we talked about the Civil War, and the Victorian morals, and the first train to Seattle, and the terrible pride of Woodrow Wilson, and the beginning of the strect car era, and the joy of not cooking, and the poems of T.S. Eliot. She died a few days later, as naturally as the melting snow.

> For brief as water falling will be death,
> and brief as flower falling, or a leaf,
> brief as the taking, and the giving, breath;
> thus natural, thus brief, my love, is death.

My education continued with the deaths of several elderly people in the church. I was always amazed at their attitude and manner. In almost every instance there was an initial anger or regret, but it was quickly followed by a calm acceptance of the inevitable and an absolute serenity at the end. How much I learned from their faith and courage is impossible to describe.

One member of the church was a very small and delicate person whom everyone tried to protect. When the doctors diagnosed her illness as terminal, it was decided, with the family, that she would not be told. I received a call, asking me to visit, but warning that I should say nothing to the patient about her condition.

Since she was weak and heavily sedated, our conversation was very brief. We talked about the weather, the church, the food at the hospital — anything to avoid the illness. Finally, I took her hand in mine and said:

> "I'll see you tomorrow."
> "I won't be here tomorrow."
> "Would you like to talk about it?"
> "No. But I'm not afraid. I'm just tired."
> "Would you like me to stay?"
> "No. I'm going to sleep."
> "Good-night."
> "Good-night. Thanks!"

She died the next day. Somehow, during the night or early morning hours, she managed to write a personal check which she left on the dresser. It was her pledge to the church for the remainder of the year. It was the last act of a neat and tidy soul.

> *Some say that gleams of a remoter world*
> *Visit the soul in sleep, that death is slumber,*
> *And that its shapes the busy thoughts outnumber*
> *Of those who wake and live.*

So I slowly began to change my own attitude in regard to death. In the beginning, it was inconceivable to me that anyone could face the crisis of death with so much dignity.

> Isn't there more rage, envy, resentment that others still have the gift of life?
> Isn't there more bitterness, depression, isolation that they have to leave this world?
> Isn't there more pain, and shock, and grief, and tears that they have to die?

But I was constantly surprised. And not only by the elderly!

I had known the couple for over a year. The husband, from Sierra Leone, was a medical student at Harvard University. The wife, a fascinating personality, had been born in London. When they joined the church, everyone was tremendously pleased — not only because they had moved so quickly from African Anglicanism to American Unitarianism — but also because they were very lovely people. They were expecting a child.

The husband called in the late afternoon. He said that his wife had just given birth to a five pound baby girl, but that the baby had died. When I arrived at the hospital, the husband and wife were sitting silently in the corner of the room, with their arms embracing each other. "It was a beautiful baby," she said. "It only lived a minute!" We cried together — and then went home.

Into a world where children shriek like suns
sundered from other suns on their arrival,
she stared, and saw the waiting shape of evil,
so fresh her understanding, and so fragile.

Oh, let us do away with pietistic
drivel! Who can restore a thing so brittle,
so new in any jingle? Still I marvel
that, making light of mountainloads of logic,
so much could stay a moment in so little.

I finally learned, after several years of living with the dying, that death is not frightening, horrible, the monster so many wish to avoid. In almost every patient, it enters quietly. It is like a silent rain. It is even welcomed!

For if a patient has been given some help in working through the initial turmoil, he will reach a plateau during which he is no longer concerned with his "fate." In the view of Kubler-Ross:

He will have mourned the impending loss of people and places, and he will contemplate his coming end with expectation.

He will be tired and weak, and he will have an increasing need to extend the hours of sleep, very similar to that of the new-born child.

He will wish to be left alone, or at least not bothered by the outside world, and he will prefer a loving hand to all conversation.

He will then die in a state of acceptance, an existence without fear or despair, and he will sink back into the egg of night.

Anyone who has sat with a dying person in the silence that goes beyond words, knows that this moment is neither hideous nor painful, but a peaceful sigh of the body. Watching such a death reminds us of a falling star; one of the million lights in a vast sky that flares up for a brief moment only to disappear into the mystery of space.

One of my most memorable experiences was with a prominent surgeon, who had been informed that he had only a year to live. His home was far out in the marshes of southern New England, where he could escape the tension of his profession and relax in the rhythm of nature. He was truly a Renaissance figure — with an interest in everything.

In one of our conversations, I asked him bluntly:

"Why do you never show anger at your condition?"

"Because I always expected it, sooner or later."

"Then you're not afraid of death?"

"Hell, no! I've seen too much to be afraid."

"I often wondered what you would tell the family when someone has died on your operating table."

"I say that living is always more difficult than dying."

The words of a man who was not a cynic, or a pessimist, or suicidal — but absolutely in love with life. It was only that he saw death as the logical conclusion, with no shade of panic or fear.

> *I have a rendezvous with Death*
> *At some disputed barricade,*
> *When spring comes back with rustling shade*
> *And apple-blossoms fill the air.*

I remember them all.

The immigrant cabinet-maker, who refused all help from anyone. His only wish was to die at home.

The recluse millionaire, whom no one thought was still living. She gave all her money to her dogs.

The affable lawyer, who always enjoyed a Sunday laugh. He asked that *Peanuts* be read at his grave.

The lonely widow, who had always been terrified at death. When she died, it was an anti-climax.

The loyal secretary, who always helped others. She died alone, so that no one would be bothered.

The old man, who lived to be 97 on a quart of bourbon every day. We drank to him 'til midnight!

All of them — and many more. They were the greatest of teachers.

So I have learned a great deal from my ministry to the dying, which has helped to place my own personal fears in a healthy perspective.

I have learned that a single human life is the most precious entity in all of God's creation, not to be bartered for a wish or a king's fortune.

I have learned that our mysterious existence on earth is too much filled with petty thoughts, with trivial concerns, and with meanness toward our fellow creatures.

I have learned that it is good to live with a knowledge of our own finitude, to live as if each moment is our last, so that what we do is a new kind of doing.

I have learned that the fear of death, which arises largely from our personal fantasies and cultural anxieties, is more to be dreaded than death itself.

And I have also learned that the human being is a marvelous construction, with the strength, and the courage, and the faith to confront any power in the universe — even the Reaper, whose name is Death.

I will always remember my last conversation with a delightful middle-aged woman, who had the capacity to find humor in every situation. It was in a nursing home, where she had about a week to live.

She whispered: "I'm going up to Heaven to meet my husband."

I said: "Which husband, Esther? You've been married three times."

And she replied: "My fourth!"

The Resurrection

The old man was weary.

As he sat leaning against the fountain in the small square of the city, his body seemed limp and lifeless. He was exhausted from the long night's journey to Jerusalem, and from the three-hour watch in the burning sun on the hill.

He was also the victim of a deeper anguish, but the excited voices of the gathering pilgrims would provide no rest. Since he could not move, and he could not sleep — he listened.

One voice was crude and boastful:

"So I yelled up at him: 'Sir, if you really are of the supernatural, then give us some supernatural sign or miracle!' You see, I had heard all those stories: changing water to wine, walking on the lake, healing the sick.

So I yelled up at him: 'Sir, if you cannot save Israel, then why not save yourself? Bring the lightning down! Open up the heavens! Disappear in a cloud of glory!' Is it not true that Elijah went to heaven in a chariot?

So I yelled up at him: 'Come on, Messiah! Your move now! We are waiting for a sign!' After all, seeing is believing, and miracles don't happen every day. But he never saw the humor, and died with all the soldiers laughing."

"An evil and adulterous generation seeks for a sign . . ." thought the old man to himself. It was a saying he had remembered from the man on the cross. So many had wanted magic.

Another voice was cool and proud:

"But really, the man was ignorant. He had no proper

parents; he had no formal education; he had no knowledge of philosophy. He was merely a provincial — a peasant preacher with insufferable pretensions to learning.

I would have relished a debate. I would have said: 'I think, sir, that if you are the truth, then it will be a rational truth that you represent. Could you please demonstrate the rational wisdom behind your arguments?' For what did that poor fellow know of logic?

No, the real Messiah will be the ultimate philosopher. He will present a solid, unifying, objective principle of authority — not homey rhymes and childish riddles. For more than anything, we must put our faith in reason. It is the only truth worth knowing.

The old man opened his eyes to confirm the Greek origin of the last speaker. Seeing the clean white skin, the well-shaved head, and the gold-embroidered gown, he winced out of instant recognition and disgust. He knew the Greeks were now the slaves of Rome. They lectured endlessly.

Another voice was harsh and violent:
"You cowards! Take comfort in your superstitions! Take comfort in your wisdom! Take comfort in your wine and women! Have you learned nothing from the years of Roman tyranny? We must fight to win our freedom!

In Isaiah it is written: 'The government shall be upon his shoulders: and his name shall be called Wonderful Counselor, Mighty God, Everlasting Father. Upon the throne of David he will sit, to establish it with judgment, and with righteousness from henceforth even forever.'

Yes, the fool on the cross is a laughing-stock. But I will put my confidence in the strength of my hands; I will put my trust in the clash of arms; and I will put my faith in the point of a blade! The King will come, and our enemies will be scattered in the dust!"

A hush fell upon the gathering, as the people were unnerved by the radical words of the zealot. Such speech in Jerusalem was punishable by death, and spies were everywhere. The old man pretended sleep. He had no strength for violence.

The next voice was timid and afraid:

"Well, for me, life is just real good the way it is. I mean, I don't know why we have to have messiahs, and saviors, and wars — or anything. I mean, why do we have to be unfriendly?

I mean, I have a wife and children whom I value most highly. I have nice friends and neighbors whom I treat with great respect. I have a lovely home with terraced gardens and fruit in season, and wines from seven kingdoms. I mean, what more could I want?

I mean, I don't usually speak up like this, but can't we all be friends? I have nothing against Herod, or Pilate, or the man on the cross — or anyone. I mean, I think we should all be thankful — and not change anything. Do you think I said something important?"

"No," thought the old man. For his legs ached, and his heart was pounding through his robe. He had no friends or family, no wines or garden, no peace of mind or hope in the future — and that is why he had come to Jerusalem. The old man had nothing, but a memory and a question.

Another voice was silly and vacuous:

"Well spoken! I always say that love is most important! Oh, 'tis love that makes the world go round — go round — go round! Love is the answer. Love! Love! Love!

Listen, friends: It doesn't matter what you believe, as long as you're sincere. I told a man the other day: 'I'm not interested in your faith, your politics, or your morals — as long as you're sincere.' I always say that to people! Every day — in every way!

Now why do you suppose that man was crucified today? It was because he was not sincere! We should all simply love, and hug, and kiss each other! Right? I almost shouted up at him: 'Be sincere! Love each other!' But I arrived too late for him to hear."

The old man groaned, as he moved slightly to shift his weight against the fountain. The light was almost gone, and many of the pilgrims were departing to find rooms for the night.

A passing voice was young and earnest:

"But I think they have forgotten the art of politics. You see, philosophy is just abstraction. Violence is irrational. Pleasure leads to weakness. Love is a sentimental gesture without purpose or design.

You see, the real Messiah will appear with a viable program for the New Tomorrow. How, exactly, do we eliminate poverty? How, exactly, do we reform government? How, exactly, do we establish justice? What we need is a social program that will answer those questions.

You see, I think the Messiah, perhaps a scribe or a librarian, will produce such an outline for the New Society. He will devise a lofty code or ethical principles, a sanctified system of moral law, and a practical program of social and political reform. You see — I think we will know him by his plan. You see?"

When suddenly, a black robe appeared on the edge of the square, and in its height, and width, and depth seemed to fill the sky with darkness. The old man blinked at the threatening apparition.

A voice screamed at the pilgrims:

"Blasphemy! Blasphemy! Was not the creature on the cross a lesson to you all? Did you not see him bleed and die like a dumb animal? Must God blind you, or cripple you, or strike you dead to make you understand?

Truth is not something born with you like hair and bones! Truth is not something distributed among you like seeds and flowers! Truth is in the ancient tradition! Truth is in the sacred ritual! Truth is in the rites of your fathers, ordained from the beginning of time!

You despise your fathers? You forsake your traditions? You break the laws? Then go to the High Priest! Go to the Temple! Go to the Holy of Holies! Get down on your knees, and pray for forgiveness! Beg for mercy! Our God is a jealous God — and the fear of Him is the beginning of wisdom!"

The thundering words of the priest were followed by a flurry of voices:

"It's very late."

"I have a room — good night!"

"Must rise early tomorrow."

"Good-bye."

"Good night!"

As the crowd dispersed, darkness appeared. The three crosses on the hill, once visible from the fountain, were now lost in the evening shadows. The old man gasped for breath, and realized that he could not move his body. Then, all was silent.

"Is it finished?" he thought.

The mind swept back to another night, long ago, when the sky was clear of clouds, and a bright star burned in the heavens. It remembered the crowds of pilgrims and the travelers from distant lands. It remembered a young couple, who could not find room at the Inn. It remembered the stable, the manger, and the new-born child in swaddling clothes. It remembered the visitors: shepherds, wisemen, and kings.

"What a glorious beginning," it thought.

Then the mind rushed forward three decades in time, ignoring all the events of a mundane and faithless existence, in a delirious search for a final meaning. It remembered the news of two days ago, that a man named "Jesus of Nazareth" was to be crucified in Jerusalem. It remembered the shock of recognition and the dreadful pain of a guilty conscience. It remembered the long journey to the foot of the cross on the hill, and it remembered the words: "Forgive them, Father, for they know not what they do."

"Who was he?" it thought. "Was he the Messiah?"

Then all thought ended.

In the morning, the two soldiers found a body slumped against the fountain in the square. It was an old man.

When they searched his few belongings, they were able to discover his identity:

Name: "John"

Residence: "Bethlehem"

Occupation: "Inn-keeper"

Chapter IV

Greet One Another With a Holy Kiss

> "To communicate with Mars, converse with spirits,
> To report the behavior of the sea monster,
> Describe the horoscope, haruspicate or scry,
> Observe disease in signatures, evoke
> Biography from the wrinkles of the palm
> And tragedy from fingers; . . ."
> — T. S. ELIOT

Should I Swim To Honolulu?

Dear Helen:

I received your letter yesterday, in the rush of writing my final sermon before summer vacation. Since we are strangers, it was useful to learn that you are single, twenty-three years old, a college graduate, a Unitarian-Universalist, and a resident of Mount Vernon, Iowa. I, too, have known all of those human experiences, though, thank God, never at the same time!

While not demeaning your personal predicament, I am compelled to inform you that I receive almost fifty letters a year from people interested in moving to San Francisco.

Many are inquiring about housing or employment;

Many are worried about climate or earthquakes;

Many are concerned about crime or cultural shock.

But most are written from the small towns and cities of the United States with the visionary goal of finding a new life in the "Dream City" of America.

As a liberal minister, who has looked for the Holy Grail while living in six states and nine cities, I have come to doubt the principle of salvation through geography.

If you are an unhappy person in Bangor, you will be
an unhappy person in San Francisco.

If you are a lousy person in Butte, you will be
a lousy person in San Francisco.

If you are a creepy person in Baton Rouge, you will be
a creepy person in San Francisco.

I have never met anyone who was fundamentally changed by geography. It is said that even Buzz Aldrin carried his problems to the moon!

I remember, when I first arrived in the Bear State, people

kept asking the question: "How do you suppose California is going to change you?" When I replied:

that I did not need to be changed;

that I did not want to be changed;

and that I would rather change California —

I was met with those incredulous stares usually reserved for the vilest heretics. (It is an article of faith in California that everyone needs to be changed.)

As I write this letter, Helen, I am reminded of a young man I met who was very depressed.

He had submitted to the pressure for sailing, jogging, capping his teeth, and developing a healthy tan.

He had consumed tons of bean-sprouts, raisins, sesame seeds, and natural peanut butter.

He had lived indiscriminately in a Residence House, a Commune, a Singles Apartment, and a boat in Sausalito.

He had joined a local Mud Bath, a Rolfing Clinic, a Primal Scream Spa, and a Karate Institute.

Yet nothing seemed to work. He was still lonely, alienated, and depressed.

Finally, one day, I said to the young man:

"You know, everything you do is inner-directed, self-serving, and egotistical. Have you ever thought that you might best improve your condition, not by pampering the ego, but by sacrificing the ego? Try reaching out to other human beings without tricks, or games, or gimmicks — but with real sincerity and compassion."

Having tried everything else, he began working as a volunteer in a nursing home. Today, he is studying to be a male nurse at a local hospital, with little depression and no more puka shells.

Not all stories end so well.

The image of people in California as being well-adjusted, easy-going, and fun-loving is a Hollywood fantasy. Depression is a billion dollar industry in the Promised Land, and the recently uprooted young are easy prey for the hucksters of salvation. The exotic merry-go-round of activity is often only a denial of the basic self, as meditation and nude bathing will hardly enlighten an empty mind.

I say this not as an enemy of California, but only to lower your expectations. Our Jesuit, Zen-Buddhist, Napoleonic Governor is much in favor of lowered expectations.

Since you are inquiring specifically about San Francisco, however, I should say a word about the city, which denies any relationship to California as a whole. I have just finished reading *The Diary* of James Boswell, the 18th Century biographer. He wrote:

> *I have often amused myself with thinking how different a place London is to different people. They, whose narrow minds are contracted to the consideration of some one particular pursuit, view it only through that medium. But the intellectual man is struck with it, as comprehending the whole of human life in all its variety, the contemplation of which is inexhaustible.*

What a marvelous sentiment for those in love with cities! I agree wholeheartedly.

Personally, I have never cared for Jefferson's intellectual rejection of cities, and his dream of an ideal republic of self-reliant farmers — a pathetic dream for a good and great man whose land was tilled by slaves. In real life, the Medieval peasant and the Modern rural commune are the least free of people: bound by nature, ridden by caste, fettered by group norms, and riddled by suspicion and foreboding of whatever is new and different.

"City air makes free," was the Medieval saying; and city air still makes free the runaways from factory towns, from small farms, from mining villages, and from one-class suburbs. It may be romantic to search for the salves of society's ills in the backwaters of Oregon and Idaho, or among the innocent, unspoiled farmers of Maine (if such exist), but it is a waste of time. Does anyone really suppose that the answers to any of the great questions that plague us today are going to be found in Pittsville, U.S.A.?

Incidentally, I often joke with the Church Staff about their preference for the country. They are always rushing off to the lakes and mountains with a primitive gleam in their eyes.

I tell them that the closest I ever lived to nature was at a Holiday Inn in Fresno.

I tell them that it took one million years to invent the bathroom, so why should I revert to the monkey?

I tell them that I refuse to play golf because I never learned to walk on grass.

Yet, seriously, I also believe that nature watching is more instructive in the city than in the country. All one has to do is to accept *homo sapiens* as a part of Nature. It is better than a swarm of mosquitoes in a leaky tent!

So if you enjoy and appreciate the rhythm and diversity of cities, you will "lose your heart in San Francisco." Admittedly, the appeal of the city is subtle and mysterious. After all:

> It leads the nation in major crime;
> It leads the nation in alcoholism;
> It leads the nation in suicides.

> New York has better theatre;
> Boston has better universities;
> Louisville has a better newspaper.

> The public schools are atrocious;
> The professional sports are parodies;
> The cost of living is flagrant thievery.

Also, as in most large cities, much of the charm has been lost to the demands of business, labor, and the real estate developers — who have chosen to build skyscrapers that are marvels of dullness and regimentation, and cultural centers that are unable to support a good bookstore.

Ah, but with all the problems, I have never known a more seductive city than San Francisco.

> It is more than the climate — mild in the summer and mild in the winter — with flowers blooming the year around.
> It is more than the devilish houses, teetering on the cliffs and ravines, like so many boxes with legs.
> It is more than the twenty-four hundred restaurants, serving every variety of taste the world has ever known.
> It is more than the sound of the ocean smashing the rocks at the Golden Gate, or washing the sands at Baker Beach.
> It is more than the human patchwork of every conceivable color, and texture, and style, and direction.
> It is even more than the attitudes of freedom, openness, and toleration for which the city is proudly noted.

Yes, Helen, the attraction of the city is much more profound than what the tourist can readily grasp.

> I think it has something to do with being so isolated, situated in a western location so far from the mainstream of America.
> I think it has something to do with being a peninsula, situated on a piece of land almost completely surrounded by water.

I think it has something to do with being so vulnerable,
   situated on one of the most dangerous earthquake faults
   in the world.
And if the people of San Francisco do not talk a great deal about
their isolation, their encirclement, and their vulnerability — it
is, nonetheless, the unconscious motivation for much of our
behavior.

Think of the ancient city of Pompeii! Why was it the most
fabulous city in the Roman Empire? Why did it attract the
adventurous young from every province? Why did its streets
flourish with artists and artisans? Why was it so free, and open,
and tolerant? Why did it charm the curious tourists? What was
the mysterious appeal of Pompeii? Only that it lay isolated in
southern Italy, on the Bay of Naples, at the foot of Mount
Vesuvius!

In a city of people who have surrendered their roots in favor
of a life of risk and daring, it is like living in the last days: as
some turn to crime, drugs, or suicide; as others turn to cults,
magic, or superstition; and still others turn to love, play, or
creativity. Yet, in such a time and in such a place, the boundaries
of human experience are extended, the intensity of thought and
emotion is increased, and the warmth of our brothers and sisters
is more desperately needed. We live more fully — and more
dangerously!

Is it a curse or a blessing? I should think only that it is
necessary.

If San Francisco did not exist on the far western reaches of
   the continent, it would have to be invented by the gods.
If the Garden of Eden was a place of order, obedience, and
   serenity, then there must be a place for change, protest,
   and fluidity.
If there are people, anywhere, strangled by the roots of tradition and prejudice, they must be given the opportunity
   to breathe the heady air of freedom.
You see, Helen, in all societies, there needs to be a city at the
foot of Vesuvius. For it sharpens the joys and sorrows, portrays
the good and evil, and serves ultimately the interest of all society
— in pointing to the edge!

Obviously, I hope you do not take my remarks to be anything
more than the general impressions of a transplanted Easterner.
Indeed, without knowing you better, I can offer no special insight
as to why you should leave or stay in Mount Vernon, Iowa. I can

only wish you the very best in making that personal decision.

In the meantime, I must reluctantly conclude this letter.

I see the sun is streaming through the fog on Twin Peaks;

I have some deer skin loafers and a gold chain necklace;

I purchased a king-size waterbed and a small lemon tree;

I stored a bushel of avocados and several quarts of good
cheap wine;

I consulted my horoscope and the bio-rhythm chart;

and I am prepared for a long vacation.

Yes, Helen, in some ways I, too, am a convert. The moth is ever attracted to the flame — but what a glorious flight!

Sincerely,

David O. Rankin

> "The young dead soldiers do not speak.
> Nevertheless, they are heard in the still
> houses: who has not heard them? . . . They
> say: We were young. We have died . . .
> Remember us."
> — ARCHIBALD MACLEISH

A Dead Soldier Looks at the War

Dear Mother and Father:

My deepest apologies for not writing more often. Time lies heavy here — but it is not well used in writing or thinking. Please believe me when I say that home has never been so dear. I love you.

My present assignment is in a small village in the hills to the south of the capital. Our unit has the duty of searching out and destroying enemy concentrations in the countryside.

Let no one tell you of the glories of war! I no longer have the illusions of a raw recruit. All of the men are weary. Most of the men complain. No one wants to die. The morale is high, if only in order to survive. That is the point now — the only point — to survive. It is the only glory!

I have learned that this small forsaken land, halfway around the world, is part of a very old world. Our own history is but a single page when compared to the long story of these ancient people. It is a ceaseless flow of events, timeless, with no real beginning and nothing to end.

Yet, by our lights, the conditions are primitive and the people backward. Pure water is a luxury. A soft bed is a dream. Most villages have no sanitation. Despite official claims, starvation is still rampant. All our efforts to improve the conditions, to train the natives, to raise the standard of living, and to reform the government — all have amounted to nothing. Only the rich get richer.

I suppose war and good intentions can never co-exist. We destroy towns and build villages. We slaughter young men and educate their children. We spread disease and distribute medicines. We burn forests and plant small trees. The noble purpose does not keep pace with the intense destruction. It is a costly lesson.

The enemy are not professionals. Most prisoners are fifteen to nineteen years old. Ten and twelve-year-olds are not uncommon. Many are women. I have seen them myself.

While this is a reluctant confession, quite recently formed, I have come to respect them. They are not well trained or equipped. They are young and small in stature. Yet, they are absolutely fanatical, extremely loyal, and virtually unyielding in combat. Then, too, they believe they are fighting for a righteous cause — for the freedom and independence of their homeland. There is no dissuading them.

I have finally accepted the status of foreigner. It was not easy at first, to meet the cold stares of the people — which express such an obvious hatred and open hostility for an army of liberation. The great majority do not want us here. They do not want this war. They are merely caught in the rush of great events.

Most of the villagers do not even take sides. How can they? Why should they? The enemy butchers whole families. We destroy their crops and animals. The enemy are without honor and decency. We are the allies of a weak and corrupt ruler. So the people suffer patiently while others decide their fate. They bear the burden of all wars. Still, I would have liked to have won their respect. Now even that is gone.

Is it not sad that the judgment of history comes long after the participants are dead? I mean: the statesmen, the soldiers, the civilians . . . everyone is gone before history determines the reasons, the meanings, the effects, and the justice of it all. Do you understand?

I dread thinking all of this will be a mere footnote in a dry historical document . . . a meaningless affair. The actors should know the script before the play begins. Perhaps we do — but play our roles to the bitter end.

The troops received a directive today. Over one-third of the men have caught disease from the local women. We have been told "the only permanent relief for the mating urge can be obtained through speeding the victory and return to home." Many of us feel it is a better reason for fighting than all the others advanced.

I knew the people at home had doubts about this war from the very beginning, so I am not surprised it has become increasingly unpopular. But the old men who plan our wars will not be moved by youthful protest. For centuries they have sent armies out, with regularity, to dictate, control, or conquer. It has become a privilege of old age. The youthful demonstrators of today are the old men of tomorrow.

Forgive the cynicism. It is a soldier's luxury. We know nothing about the war. There are no lectures here. No speeches — no debates. Just the drab, miserable, wasted faces of men who know only how to die.

I am not disloyal. I condemn no one (or is it everyone?). I have no solutions. I am just here. We are all just here. Our eyes still see; our hands still move; our hearts still beat . . . but we do not know if we are still alive.

Many of us wonder what it will be like to come home. We fear peace as well as war. We have no skills. We are weary and broken. We are older, not wiser — but changed. Others will not understand us.

What life is there after the crucible of war? I remember the soldiers from the last war. The welcome! The marching through the streets! The cheers! Then, as the years passed: the pot-bellies, the ludicrous caps, the worn-out stories. A veteran is more pitiful than a whore.

But perhaps it is all mere melancholy! When I return, I will once again sit in the sun and listen to the children play. I will laugh again. I will dream again. I will love again. The noise of battle, the ugliness of war, the smell of the dead . . . all will pass away with the whisper of the wind.

I cannot predict the end. We exist amidst hope and despair; between rumors of peace and talk of a larger war; between orders for a troop withdrawal and orders for a renewed offensive; between news of great victories and knowledge of crushing defeats. We have that much in common with the peasants. We, too, are caught in the middle of a gigantic puzzle. I think the end will come when everyone is bored.

Do you remember, Mother, how I used to tremble as a child when a human life was in danger? There was nothing greater — nothing more sacred than life. Yet, here, life is wasted and worthless. Flesh is cheap. Blood is free. Only the dead are counted here. All wars are a contest of the dead.

Yesterday, I came upon a body in the field. It had grown rigid in death and appeared like a grotesque statue. In the pocket of the vest I found a note, wet and stained, which read: "Let us turn our faces to the earth. Let us sleep upon our laurels. Nothing makes any difference." I noticed two medals on the chest. They had not stopped the bleeding.

We are not yet civilized! With all our learning, with all our discoveries, with all our achievements — the human race is still in its infancy. The future will write comedies of our history. We are still savages and cannibals who eat our own. A change *must* come — but when? I do not know.

It is time to rest. Tonight, we go out to seek the enemy. What a game to play!

Please extend my greetings to old friends and, of course, my love to all the family. I miss you terribly.

I love you.

Post-script:

As I lay thinking about this letter, I realize how it may shock you, or cause dismay, or pity. My first thought is to burn it — and to begin another in a manner more pleasant.

But you, of all people, must know that I cannot lie or feign good humor. Already, there is too much pretending.

I do have hope. I have not mentioned hope. But through all the disillusionment, through all the horror, through all the regrets of yesterday and the fears of tomorrow — it persists and gives me strength. A man without hope is only a latent force, only a possibility, like a stone waiting for the blow from the iron to give forth sparks. A man without hope is dead.

What I lack is faith. Is not this the missing element? What our generation needs is the inspiration, the stimulus, that will turn hope into reality. What we desperately lack as a people is the spiritual force that will provoke us to implement our rational solutions with kindness and tenderness. What we need is the passionate allurement, the daring courage, and the risk-taking spirit of a bold new faith. Is it possible? I do not know.

But I am amused and heartened that even here, among the poor peasants, in these dark times and in this infested land, there are signs of such a faith.

The other day, an old villager disclosed that a child will be born — "A Lamb of God," he called him. In time, he will change men's hearts, establish justice on the earth, and bring peace to all the world.

"Hosanna! Hosanna!" I replied in his native tongue. "O save! Save, we pray thee!"

Your Son,
Marcus Sentilius
Servant of Rome
in Bethlehem
of Judea

In The Beginning . . . God

Dear Son:

In the gospel according to *Peanuts,* little Linus and Charlie Brown are sitting together, in the dark, in the middle of a pumpkin patch. Linus is anxiously awaiting the arrival of the "Great Pumpkin," who will bring gifts and toys and candy. Charlie Brown is a skeptic — like you.

After a time, a small head is seen in the dark and Linus yells, "There he is! There he is! It's the Great Pumpkin! He's rising out of the pumpkin patch!" In the excitement, he faints.

A few seconds later, Linus is revived. He looks at Charlie Brown and Snoopy. "What happened? Did he leave us any toys?" "No toys," says Charlie Brown, "just a used dog."

But Linus can never believe that it was only Snoopy in the shadows. His faith unshaken, in the final caption he looks to the sky, waves his hand, and says: "He must be well on his way by this time. Happy journey, O Great Pumpkin! Happy journey!"

As I recall, my own childhood religion was very similar to that of Linus. If I did not sit in the pumpkin patch, I did inherit a view of God that was based on my needs and yearnings. For I was taught that God was a wonderful Being in the sky, who created the earth and the universe out of nothing; who answered prayers and petitions with alarming speed; who fought against evil and eliminated suffering; and who smiled with love and compassion on all human creatures. Those were the happy and secure years!

However, "when I was a child, I spoke as a child, I understood as a child, I thought as a child: but when I became a man, I put away childish things." Or did they simply vanish? I think it is much more accurate — for I did not will them away. Whatever happened to Howdy Doody? Whatever happened to Santa Claus? Whatever happened to God? Like the smile of the Cheshire Cat — they simply disappeared!

For the next ten years, I totally rejected the idea of God as incompatible with the real world. When asked to express my beliefs:

> I could easily quote Sigmund Freud to the effect that God is purely a creation of the human imagination, a childish fairytale for the ignorant and confused.
> I could blithely quote Bertrand Russell to the effect that God is a referent which is no longer credible in light of scientific, philosophical and historical studies.
> Or, I could passionately quote Karl Marx to the effect that God is a tool of the wealthy and the powerful, which is used like an opiate to keep the poor in the bonds of slavery.

My heavens! I was smart! And I taught Political Science from a secular perspective; I worked in the community as an ethical humanist; and I had nothing to do with organized religion. Those were the sure and confident years!

In the early 1960's, however, I began to experience a profound change in my life: a feeling of not being whole; a feeling of not being complete; a feeling of not being in touch with the real. It gushed forth in a series of doubts which flooded my mind and shattered my confidence. The questions were similar to those you have raised.

> Who am I?
> Where am I going? What is the meaning of life?
> What is evil?
> Where is the source of values? Is death the only reality?
> What is knowledge without purpose?
> Is suffering necessary?
> How can I love myself? What is the mystery of creation?
> Do I know anything at all?

While some could live in the midst of meaninglessness and absurdity; while some could react with heroic bitterness and revulsion; and while still others could find sufficient satisfaction in their daily round of activity not to miss or lament the dimension of depth and mystery — I could hardly survive. Those were the shaken and disturbed years!

During the next period, I was introduced to my own ignorance: regretfully, unhappily, and painfully. It was Paul Tillich who best described my condition when he wrote:

Anxiety about meaninglessness is the characteristically human form of ontological anxiety. It is the form of anxiety which only a being can have in whose nature freedom and destiny are united. The threat of losing this unity drives man toward the question of the infinite, unthreatened ground of meaning; it drives him to the question of God.

And sure enough: the more I studied philosophy, the closer I was driven to metaphysics; and the more I studied metaphysics, the closer I was driven to theology; and the more I studied theology, the closer I was driven to God.

It was a marvelous process of discovery — lasting many years.

In the first place, I had never fully realized that the concept of God was a universal phenomenon, not limited to a particular age, or culture, or people.

Ikhnaton, an Egyptian pharaoh, spoke of God as "that which fashions the beauty of form through thyself alone. For thou art the Lord of the day and thou art in my heart."

Aristotle, a Greek philosopher, defined God as "the First Mover, upon which depend the heavens and the world of nature, a living being, eternal, and most good."

Gandhi, an Indian reformer, saw God as "the mysterious power that pervades everything which I gather is Life, Truth, Light. God is love — the Supreme Good."

And Helen Keller, a blind American, experienced God as "the beauty and harmony of the real world. God is in all that liberates and lifts, in all that humbles, sweetens and consoles."

So, in turning the pages of history, I learned that the conception of God is the product of a long and tortuous struggle, and has been shaped by the experience and reflection of many peoples. What has been handed down is the work of the collective imagination of generations of men and women who have been deeply involved with their whole being: primitive hunters in the bush of Australia; tribes of nomads on the Mongolian Steppes; kings and queens on the thrones of Europe; and nuclear physicists in the silence of outer space. Here was the verification of my own experience! I learned I was not alone!

In the second place, I had never fully appreciated the function of God for an understanding of the world. You see, I demanded a rational system, without magic, riddles, and miracles — a sophisticated orientation that would not contradict the evidence of the senses.

> I knew that Plato and Aristotle had introduced the concept of God as an intellectual necessity for their descriptions of reality.

> I knew that St. Augustine and St. Thomas had posited a Creator as an indispensable ingredient for the understanding of existence.

> I knew that Kant and Spinoza had argued for the logical requirement of God for any serious analysis of human behavior.

> And, I knew that Schweitzer and Einstein had both claimed their philosophies were influenced by an ultimate reality found at the heart of the universe.

But it was Alfred North Whitehead — the dry mathematician turned dry theologian — who supplied the missing links.

I was excited by Whitehead! His argument for the existence of God is primarily the traditional one from the order of the universe to a ground of order. He writes:

> *I cannot understand the world apart from God . . . There is a deep human intuition that the order of the world requires for its explanation – some principle of order that cannot entirely be attributed to the entities that constitute the world. . . . That there is something which we may properly call God is sufficiently indicated by the kind of order that is visible to all."*

It is difficult reading. But the significance of Whitehead lies in the unusual thoroughness of his work, and in the fact that it does justice to the complexities of modern physics, as well as to the arguments of modern skeptics. Here was a theology that did not surrender the rational faculty! I learned I was not a fool!

In the last place, the most important, I had never fully explored my own personal relationship to God. I suppose I was too heavily influenced by the psychological fads of the era, as everything was interpreted through Freudian, Rogersian, or Maslowian scriptures. I had to probe deeper.

> I began to attend church again: learning the discipline of prayer, joining in the hymns of celebration, reading the poetry of the ages, and participating in a community of faith.

I began to practice a daily meditation, which I had learned
from Eckhart and St. John, in order to seek, identify,
and relate to the sources of the Holy that lie at the
deepest level of consciousness.

I began to strip away the small lies, the large pretensions,
the intellectual pride, and the defensive mechanisms
which had served to block the flow of feeling and to
deny the intuitive realities.

I began to be frightened, as I sensed my own finiteness, guilt,
despair, and realized that I was a helpless, limited being
in a world not of my making, and ultimately out of my
control.

But then I began to perceive a mysterious power and energy,
at times awesome and tremendous, at times smooth and
comforting, like the perpetual murmur of the waves
beyond the shore.

And I began, slowly, to live in the world, not in rebellion
or resignation, but in the context of a larger vision of
value, meaning, and purpose which I could accept as
Divine.

It was never easy. There were many doubts, many curses, many
prayers, many silences, many mistakes, many confessions, and
many fears — but those were the years of discovery and renewal!

Today, the journey is far from over, as I continue to explore
the questions that began in childhood — constantly developing
new beliefs.

I believe, for example, in the virtue of humility. For if God
is not totally accessible to the human creature, it is best
to guard against the pomposity, fanaticism, and
unctuousness of the religious posture by freely admit-
ting that everything could be completely mistaken. God
is not a possession!

I believe, for example, in the freedom of suffering. For if
God is not a genie who will solve all of the problems
of the faithful, it is better to nourish faith on the man
praying that the cup might pass, a prayer answered not
with legions of angels to rescue him, but with lonely
suffering on the cross. God is not a magician!

I believe, for example, in the liberation of faith. For if God
is the ultimate loyalty of our lives, it is best not to
worship the politics, causes, movements, therapies,
messiahs, drugs, or weapons that dominate our land-

scape — and to live in the perfect freedom of the infinite power. God is not an idol!

I believe, for example, in the love of people. For if God is the source of all beauty, truth, and goodness — it is best found in those intimate relationships which only the human animal is capable of enjoying — in the care, the affection, the compassion — which seem to be our highest achievement. God is love!

Finally, I must not ignore the childish element that still remains in my own view of God, for there is much of Linus that never dies. Perhaps it is best expressed in the posters and greeting cards of Corita Kent, the artist and former Roman Catholic nun. She writes:

> To believe in God is to know the world is round, not flat, and there is no edge of anything.
> To believe in God is to get so attached to everything that it can't give you up.
> To believe in God is to be able to die, and not to be embarrassed.
> To believe in God is to have the great faith that somewhere, something is not stupid.

And that is the childlike, playful, humorous, and paradoxical ingredient that no faith should ever outgrow.

Yes, son — God is a pumpkin!

Forever,

Dad

Chapter V
Let Them Bring Forth Their Witnesses

Old Macdonald Had a Farm

Anyone with a formula for salvation is a fool. For the events of our lives are too complex, too varied, too unexpected — and the best moments are often unplanned. God does work in mysterious ways, not only through kings and presidents, but in the butcher, the baker, and the candlestick maker. I offer the following as evidence.

It was a hot day in the month of July, in the year 1963. I was cruising along on a sun-baked highway through central Iowa: gazing at the hogs in the fields, watching the flies splatter against the windshield, humming to the music on the radio, and dreaming about a tall glass of beer. The road was typically Midwest, which is long, straight, and narrow.

It is not true that Iowa only exists in stories by Johnny Carson, in paintings by Norman Rockwell, and in Hollywood productions with Robert Preston, statuesque blondes, and marching bands. Or is it? In the words of a native poet:

> Air as the fuel of owls. Snow
> unravels, its strings slacken. Creamed
> to a pulp are those soft gongs
> clouds were. The children
> with minds moist as willow pile
> clouds purely in their minds; thrones
> throng on a bright mud strangely
> shining. And here
> chase a hog home as a summer sun
> rambles over the ponds, and here run
> under a sky ancient as America with
> its journeying clouds. All their hands
> are ferns and abscences. Their farm homes
> on their hills are strangely childlike.

A poet probably now living in Sausalito — on a houseboat! What in the world was I doing in Iowa? God! What was anyone doing in Iowa?

A few weeks before, I had been summoned into the office of the Editor of the *North American Review*, and asked if I would mind interviewing a farmer in Coon Rapids, Iowa. I was told that Nikita Krushchev had visited the farm in 1959 — and that a follow-up interview might make a good cover story for the next edition of the magazine. Since our circulation was sagging in the Midwest (and we were a Midwestern magazine), I decided to accept the assignment.

Still, as I wilted through the 97-degree heat of central Iowa, there were many second thoughts.

> In the first place, I had been born in a city; I hated farms; and I believed in the inherent superiority of the urban life. How can you loaf on the corner on a farm?

> In the second place, I abhorred the smell of animals and their odious little sounds — I preferred carving them on a plate to seeing them running on the ground. Frenetic chickens are especially offensive.

> In the third place, I had nothing to relate to a dull old farmer beyond my knowledge of the dust-bowls and boll-weevils I had seen in *Grapes of Wrath*. Henry Fonda never did point out the difference.

So the depression of the morning did not lessen when I saw the sign looming on the highway: *Coon Rapids, Iowa — Hog Capital of the World.*

It was not surprising to learn that the "Hog Capital of the World," unlike other capitals, did not have many people. At the only gas station, I was told I could find the famous farmer at the local feed and seed store, which was easily distinguished from the other ten buildings in the one-street town. After entering and identifying myself, I was taken to a small inner office and introduced to Mr. Roswell Garst.

> Garst, when I met him, was just over seventy years of age. He was 5'10" tall, with a large oval head protruding from sloping shoulders, The body moved slowly, like a polar bear. The eyes were alert, like a fox.

> His long white hair, deeply lined face, knarled hands, and a loose fitting white shirt with wide suspenders and no tie — altogether reminded me of a politician out of *All the King's Men.*

One other characteristic was a mechanical voice. His larynx had been removed and he manipulated air through a tiny box. The booming, sometimes crackling sound, only added to his considerable presence. For the next five hours, I was the prisoner of Roswell Garst.

Born in 1893, in northwest Iowa, he had received no formal education, and appeared to have spent his early years in riotous and poorly remembered pursuits. In 1920, Garst inherited the three-hundred acre farm of his family. By 1930, he had extended the holdings to two thousand acres and he had developed a hybrid seed corn superior to any in the area. By 1959, the five thousand acre *Apple Farm* had become the most successful experimental farm in the United States, and Roswell Garst was publicized everywhere as "The American Farmer."

Garst was proud of his rural heritage. During the short drive to the farm (in an old dusty Pontiac), he informed me that civilization began with a farmer. He fondly recalled that the oldest writing ever discovered on a clay tablet was the record of a farmer's debt to a temple. With mock seriousness, he said: "Yes, farmers have always been in debt — and only a clergyman would be mean enough to write it down." Garst was a Lutheran without a church (an independent Christian), and a political progressive without a Party (a friend and neighbor of Henry Wallace).

After a walking tour of the farm, we entered the small frame house. It was clean, neat, and simply decorated. In one corner of the living room I noticed an open scrapbook, and I asked permission to read it while he prepared our lunch. It included the signatures of the Khrushchevs, Prime Minister MacMillan, Prime Minister Nehru, three American presidents, and hundreds of other visitors. A personal note from Mrs. Krushchev was an invitation to visit Russia.

"Yes, I went to Russia," he called from the kitchen. "I dropped in on Krushchev at his summer home on the Black Sea. Lovely place. Nice man. Sold him two million dollars worth of seed."

Yet Garst was more than a farmer and a salesman. He was also a philosopher, a scientist, and a humanitarian — with a wildly eccentric spirit.

When we were settled with our milk and sandwiches, he began to talk through the tiny box.

> "In the beginning, it was awful. In 1930, the average yield of corn in the United States was 26 bushels per acre. At that time there was precious little hybrid seed corn. We were afraid to plant corn early. We had no fertilizer, no insecticides, no herbicides. We had to rotate our crops and waste the land. It took one full hour of man-labor to raise one bushel of corn. We were still in the Middle Ages!"

Not fully understanding his monologue, I switched on the tape recorder and listened, as the air from his lungs formed words through the tiny hole in his neck.

> "I began to experiment in 1932. I doubled the production of corn per acre. I planted well-adapted hybrid seed corn and planted early in the season. I developed an adequate fertilizer program. I discovered a soil insecticide to kill the root-worms and atrazine, a form of weed control. It took thirty years, but today it requires less than three minutes of man-labor to raise a bushel of corn — and I have a yield of eighty bushels an acre. . . ."

As I sipped the milk, he spoke slowly — with huge gulps of air. The energy and determination of the man was truly incredible. I could understand his past victories over the soil, as I watched his current struggle with a major handicap.

> "While experimenting with animals, I discovered a nitrogen chemical called urea. It can be fed to cattle, sheep, goats, or to camels in the Middle East. It contains one hundred per cent of their needed protein and is potentially unlimited in supply. Why do one-fifth of the households in the United States have inadequate diets? Why do over sixteen million people in America suffer from hunger and malnutrition? Why does one-third of the world go to bed hungry every night? It's politics and bureaucrats! Not the failure of technology. Not the failure of the farmer!"

I finished the sandwich, but continued to listen as his voice began to weaken. He seemed to be sucking all air from the room. I yearned to give him mine.

"The population of the world CAN be well-fed, and feeding people well is one way to check the growth of population. When food is plentiful, our hopes and aspirations are a motivating factor for peace. THINK OF IT! THINK OF IT! The world spends a hundred billion dollars a year for a war no one wants — while people starve in every land. Feed the soil! Feed the crops! Feed the people! That's the way to peace!"

Not wanting to witness more strain, I searched for a question that would bring his remarks to a conclusion. "What is the primary motivation in your life?" I asked. He replied:

"I have one guiding dream in my life: To see all people with what they need to eat. I have one ambition in my life: To contribute to the research to eliminate hunger. I have one accomplishment in my life: To know it is technically feasible to feed a hungry world."

With that, the lunch and the speech were ended.

The remainder of the day was spent in relaxed conversation, a small debate over the personality of chickens, an account of his travels around the world, and a delicious steak dinner (which turned me against Vegetarianism for several years).

I departed from Coon Rapids in the evening, as the sun fell into Nebraska. For the first time, I began to smell the corn, the oats, the clover — and to appreciate the flat, rich earth of Middle America. I began to think deeply on those men and women, living out their lives on the widely scattered farms. The flickering lights from their living-room windows seemed to dance in the gathering darkness.

I composed the article in my head, between Des Moines and Cedar Rapids, along old Route 30. The next day I wrote it down and later it was published. I might only add that it resulted in the highest sales in the history of the magazine. Of course, I should also add that Roswell Garst bought two thousand copies to distribute to his friends.

In the years that followed, I never lost sight of Garst. He was often in the media (prophetic — controversial — irrepressible).

He attacked the Department of Agriculture for not properly feeding the rural poor.

He developed a method for improving agricultural production in the tropics of Latin America.

He aided in the construction of a series of fertilizer plants
in the underdeveloped nations.

Finally, when I read the news of his death, I was plunged into sadness. For I knew that a friend of the earth and all its people was gone. There was no more air to breathe. The tiny box was silent.

My thoughts flowed back to another man and to the symbols of his ministry: the Parables on Food, the Wedding Feast, the Feeding of the Five Thousand, the Last Supper. His total concern for the people's most basic needs caused them to exclaim:

"This is indeed the prophet who is to come into the world!"

And Jesus, not blind to the truth of his ministry, replied:

"Truly, truly, you seek me, not because you saw signs, but because you ate your fill of the loaves."

So, too, of a Twentieth Century American farmer, it might at last be said:

"He giveth food to all flesh . . . he giveth food to the hungry."

Grace is everywhere!

"I reject the monstrous story
that while a man may redeem the
past — a woman never can."
— HALL CAINE

The President's Wife

It all began — for her — in Lexington, Kentucky on December 13, 1818. Mary was born into a home with a fan-shaped window above the entrance, a gleam of silver on the side-board, and rich furnishings reflected in gold-framed mirrors. It was an atmosphere of grace and comfort.

When Mary Todd first met her future husband, she was living with relatives in Springfield, Illinois. At the age of 22, she was a small, pretty, slightly plump young woman with vivid coloring of blue eyes, white skin, and light chestnut hair.

One of her many suitors, Stephen A. Douglas, had written: "The sunshine in her heart was reflected in her face." And another had said: "She is the very creature of excitement, and never enjoys herself more than when in society and surrounded by a company of merry friends."

Mary was introduced to the tall, thin, raw-boned, and penniless lawyer at a dance in Springfield. When first presented, he said: "Miss Todd, I want to dance with you the worst way." After the party, Mary bubbled with laughter to her cousin Elizabeth, "And he certainly did!"

Yet it was the classical love story — where a woman of influential family, of finishing school, of the local aristocracy — remains loyal to her lover of log-cabin origins by meeting secretly and defying family opposition. It was an honest and dramatic story.

The truthful young lawyer was to tell Mary Todd, both before and after marriage, that she was the only woman he ever loved. Was it her friendly manner? Her cheerful disposition? Her gift of conversation? Whatever the reasons, there were abundant qualities to attract a slow-speaking young man who was insecure in the company of others and given at times to somber moods.

As for Mary, she was determined to marry the man she loved even though he came from poor beginnings and was, as her sister phrased it, "the plainest looking man in Springfield." Perhaps she saw a certain latent magnetism — a quality compounded of whimsical humor, interest in people, kindness, and intellectual power. Certainly, no one else had seen it.

On the evening of November 4, 1842, in the presence of a small gathering of disgruntled relatives, Abraham Lincoln and Mary Todd were married. The groom, who had engraved the wedding ring with the words, "Love is Eternal," later expressed his ideal of married life in a letter to a friend. He wrote: "You owe obligations to her, ten thousand times more sacred than any you owe to others." The bride wrote to her sister: "There never existed a more loving and devoted husband."

The young couple moved into a one-room flat in an old boarding house called the Globe Tavern. Though Abraham's absence on the judicial circuit was one of the greatest hardships of the marriage, there was much to unite them.

They discovered the delights of classical poetry.

They recited Shakespeare and Robert Burns together.

They discussed the major political issues of the day.

And they also shared a genuine love of children.

When their son Robert was born, the first of four, the little family moved out of the boarding house and purchased a small home.

It should be noted that Abraham had traits that were very exasperating, not to future historians, but to one who had to live with him. After all, slogging around in log cabins had left him ignorant of many of the details of refined existence. So Mary taught him the small social courtesies — like wearing a shirt to the dinner table; like not going around with one pants leg up and the other down; like not spitting in the fireplace.

Of a much more serious nature was the husband's mental condition. It was once described by a doctor as "hypochrondriasm," an illness characterized by low vitality, apprehensiveness, and extreme depression. One of its most marked features was excessive morbidity. It expressed itself in nightmares and in constant thoughts of death.

It was Mary, then, who was always bolstering his ego, and helping him to fight his doubts. When he was elected to Congress, she said to a reporter, "Yes, he is a great favorite everywhere. He is to be President of the United States some day." Later, during the famous Lincoln-Douglas debates for the United States Senate, she said with puckish pride: "Mr. Douglas is a very little, little giant by the side of my tall Kentuckian, and intellectually, my husband towers above him, just as he does physically." Lincoln lost the debates (and the Senate), but later gained the Presidency.

Earlier, in 1849, their second son Edward was struck down with illness. It dragged on for 52 exhausting days, until his eyes closed in endless sleep. Mary lay stunned, turning away from food, and crying for days on end. Little did she know that it was only the first small taste of tragedy.

After the Presidential Election, both Lincolns suffered from the circulation of stories and rumors, and from the criticism and envy which politics and prominence always bring. When the First Lady arrived at the White House, she received her first gift — a painting on canvass, showing Abraham with a rope around his neck, his feet chained, and his body adorned with tar and feathers. In the carriage, on the way to the Inauguration, she heard: "There goes that Illinois ape, the cursed abolitionist! But he will never come back alive!" The dark years had begun.

She had her faults. Her two worst failings were irresponsibility as to money, which kept the Lincolns permanently in debt, and a temper, which cost them many friends. It has been generally conceded, however, that both of these traits were aggravated by the strains and tensions of Washington life. It was simply too much to endure. Too much for Mary. Too much for anyone.

The entrenched society of the Capital, for example, looked down upon her as coming from "uncivilized Illinois." It was the fashion to pass around stories of her alleged crudity and lack of education. Southerners despised her as an enemy of her own people, while Northerners thought of her as a Southern spy in the White House. Even the radical element in Lincoln's own party realized that to tear down the wife was to tear down the husband. Gossip — vicious and threatening — was everywhere.

At first, Mary tried to control the storm. She accompanied her husband on trips to the front, wanting to be by his side and to nurse his despondency. She knew of his worried, sleepless nights, and noticed the lines that were etching themselves around the eyes and mouth — so she instituted a daily carriage ride for relaxation. In such ways she tried to combat his moods of depression, and it was during this period that Abraham wrote to an old friend: "My wife is as handsome as when she was a girl, and I, a poor nobody, fell in love with her; and what is more — I have never fallen out."

But, then, William the third son fell ill in 1862. In his death, the mother was wild with grief. Between long hours of hysteria, she lay stunned and prostrated. For while she had rallied from the death of Edward, her youth was now behind her; her health was impaired; and she was a target of war and slander. Mary would never quite recover from the blow.

She tried to keep up with the usual receptions and dinners at the White House;

She worked among the wounded soldiers in the hospital as a nurse's aide;

She originated a plan for a tour of the Army by the President and his family;

She convinced her husband to grant more pardons for condemned traitors and soldiers;

And she became an ardent supporter of the emancipation of slaves long before the President.

Yet, by 1864, she was a far different person from the light-hearted woman who had first arrived in Washington. The influence of personalities, momentous events, and the all-pervading tragedy of war had deeply affected her mind and body. Headaches, nausea, compulsive spending, the uncontrollable temper — were only signs of a deeper malady.

It is recorded that Mary did not wish to go to the theatre on that fateful evening. But during the Third Act, she was nestled against her husband, looking up into his face, their fingers locked together. It was her agonized screams that first told the audience what had happened. Then, she fainted.

In her agony, she prayed that night that she, too, might die. At intervals, she returned to his bedside, again to kiss him, to call him by the tender names used in intimacy through all their years together, and to beseech him to take her with him. But Mary's struggle was not yet over.

The widow left the White House in a silent departure, with scarcely a friend to say good-bye. It was then that she began the unfortunate policy of seclusion, shunning all contact with relatives and friends whose faces she wished to avoid. In one letter she wrote:

> Day by day, I miss my beloved husband more and more. How I am to pass through life without him is impossible for me to say. I must patiently await the hour when God's love shall place me by his side again. Where there are no more partings and no more tears shed. For I have almost become blind with weeping."

There were the years abroad: wandering from place to place; taking cheap, cold lodgings; suffering from headaches, rheumatic pains, respiratory infections; and obsessed with imaginary poverty. There were the rumors: that she was insane; that Abraham had never really loved her; that she had stolen the furnishings from the White House — so many rumors (all false), but firmly fixed in the public mind for a hundred years.

In 1871, the fourth son Tad fell ill with fever and died. Mary was too ill to make the journey to Springfield where Tad was placed in the tomb beside his father. She could only lament:

> One by one, I have consigned to their resting place my loved ones, and now, in this world, there is nothing left me but the deepest anguish and desolation.

Once more she fled into exile, embarking for France, and living for a time in Switzerland and Italy. She walked the floor for sleepless nights, eyeing the windows with dread of the nameless terror that might enter through them. She had diabetes. She had difficulty with her vision. She had high blood pressure. She had injured her back in a fall.

In 1879, Mary returned to the United States on the steamer *America*. Sarah Bernhardt, the French actress, was also aboard. Pathetically, while there was much commotion over Sarah's arrival, there was nothing for Mary. The small, plump, gray-haired woman stood back, out of the way (unnoticed), to make a path for the great actress. But it was almost over.

She lived for a time in a poorly furnished backroom in a bath house in New York City. When a few old friends discovered her, she was partially paralyzed, helpless, and alone. They returned her to Springfield, where she lived as an invalid in a shade-drawn room. It is said that the children playing outside would often point to the window "where the crazy woman lived."

Then, on July 16, 1882, Mary Todd Lincoln died.

A long procession of carriages followed the casket of Abraham's widow as it was borne to Oak Ridge Cemetery in Springfield, Illinois. Her small hands were folded across her breast and on her finger was a wedding ring inscribed: "Love is Eternal."

A great crowd of the curious stood by, as she was laid where she had longed to be. "When I rest again by his side, I will be comforted," she had said. "And the waiting is so long!"

The cruel years were ended. Mary had at last come home.

A Word For Love And Affection

This past week, as I was thinking about the topic of homo-sexuality, I was reminded of a book written by Gordon Allport, called *The Nature of Prejudice*, which he wrote in the early 1950's. Allport claims that we are all born into a complex and subtle web of prejudices. They are perpetuated by our culture, by our families, by our friends, by our schools; certainly by radio, television, newspapers — even the backs of cereal boxes. He warns that these prejudices into which we are born are highly resistant to change.

He tells the true story, for example, of a small child, who was told by his father, that all monopolists are evil. So the child spends the rest of his life hating people who live in Minneapolis!

Prejudice, I think, is being down on something that we're not up on. It is always the result of either fear or ignorance — or both. So when we're talking about prejudice, whether it's leveled against blacks, or women, or Chinese, or Unitarians — or homo-sexuals — we're talking about a basic fear, and our own attempt to try to preserve our individual and personal mode of existence against something that we feel to be threatening. We're talking about ignorance, because we really don't open ourselves to new information; we really don't open ourselves to new experience; we really don't open ourselves to new patterns of thinking and feeling. That is the nature of prejudice.

It occurs to me, for example, that we might be able to combat our prejudice against homosexuality by putting sex in its proper perspective. I like sex. I think sex is good, wonderful, productive, interesting — but I believe in our society we have given sexuality a prominence and importance that it really doesn't deserve.

    I think self-esteem is more important . . .

    I think love is more important . . .

    I think survival is more important . . .

Yet, if a visitor came from outer space and looked upon the United States of America, surely he would think that the most important element in our lives is sexuality.

    Gore Vidal was right in his novel, *Myra Breckinridge,* when he wrote: "We have allowed our genitals to define who and what we are." When we look upon individuals only in terms of their sexuality, we don't see them in their fullness and in their completeness as human beings — but only as objects of envy or hatred.

    Or, it occurs to me that we might be able to combat our prejudice against homosexuality by looking at the age-old oppression of gay people. In almost every society gay people have suffered a terrible persecution and oppression. In the Medieval Period, they burned homosexuals at the stake; and the little sticks they used to start the fire they called "faggots." Today, if you stand in almost any San Francisco public school yard, you'll hear that word expressed.

    Gays have suffered imprisonment, torture, mutilation, death; and even in "liberal" San Francisco, gay people still have difficulty in finding an apartment, in writing wills, in keeping their own children in a divorce settlement, and in obtaining security clearances. They are harassed by police; they are attacked by so-called "masculine" males; and the pattern of discrimination, persecution, and oppression has continued from ancient days to our own times, today. Perhaps in knowing this history, the pain, our own prejudices can be reduced.

    Or, it occurs to me that we might be able to combat our prejudice against homosexuality by looking at the views of the medical establishment. I was reading an article the other day by Charles McCabe — sort of the Norman Mailer of the *San Francisco Chronicle*. He seems to have this need to constantly express his own masculinity — and he continues to describe homosexuality as a kind of deviant behavior. Well, that is nonsense!

    In 1973, the American Psychiatric Association, meeting in convention, voted to remove homosexuality from its list of mental disorders. It recommended that all laws that were discriminatory against homosexuals in the United States be removed. It agreed that homosexuality, while different than heterosexuality, is no better, or no worse. Furthermore, the psychiatrists claimed that homosexuality represents no impairment of personality, no impairment of vocational ability, no impairment of any kind.

We don't know what causes homosexuality — we don't know what causes many things — but certainly if we study the recent medical evidence, the evidence that's available to all of us, we can determine for ourselves that our feelings about homosexuals are not based on fact, but are based on age-old prejudices come down to us from ancient scripts of ancient times.

Or, it occurs to me that we might be able to combat our prejudice against homosexuality by thinking of the gay people we have known in our lives. It is then no longer an abstraction. It's easy to have prejudices against abstractions, generalizations, stereotypes; but it's more difficult to have them against real human beings.

I remember when I was a sophomore in high school (and I really wasn't much of a student in high school) — I had a class in American History that was taught by a gay male. For the first time in my life, while sitting in his history class, I began to appreciate the people and events of the past, and to relate those events to my own life. I began to get a sense of myself — about who I was and what I am. I remember that a group of us would often go over to his home for tea and cookies, and talk about the Roman Empire, the Greek Wars, or the expansion of the American West. History became alive — history became real.

As I read today about the controversy in Dade County, Florida, and the attempt to eliminate homosexual teachers from their public schools, I can't help but think of my old professor; and I can't help but get mad at the kinds of attitudes, the kinds of prejudices that exist, that would eliminate people on the basis of their sexuality. I think of the person who was so important in my own life — a person I admired and respected so much.

I think of another young man I knew in my last ministry. In a small New England community you don't suddenly announce that you're gay. It's not like San Francisco — you keep it quiet. You live in a kind of underworld, a kind of silence, a kind of darkness — and this was certainly true of him. He joined the church, not relating too well to the people in the beginning, until one day we attended a church conference together in a large city.

When we arrived, I introduced him to a gay friend of mine, a minister; to another friend of mine, a social worker; and they introduced him to other gay people at the conference. As we were driving home, I noticed a remarkable change! He was more open, more affable, and he suddenly wanted to talk about himself — about his gayness. I think it was because he had not only met gay people within the Unitarian-Universalist church, but he also realized that other people knew that he was gay — and they didn't care. What a feeling that must have been!

The young man went on to become a very active member of a small New England church. Occasionally, I hear of him — and I know he's still experiencing the kind of freedom which our tradition offers to its members. If you know individuals, it's quite different than thinking about abstractions. Prejudice takes a new turn — a new meaning.

Or, it occurs to me that we might be able to combat our prejudice against homosexuality by looking beyond the popular stereotype. I suppose most people think that a gay male is a person who works in a beauty parlor during the day, at night puts on his black leather jacket, and then cruises the bars on Polk Street. Or, they think of the gay female as a heavy-set, butch-hair-cutted woman who teaches weight-lifting at the YWCA.

Actually, gay people deliver your mail, and your milk, and they serve you in restaurants. They are airline pilots, generals, doctors, lawyers, clergy, dentists. They are carpenters, and plumbers, and electricians. Almost 25 million people in our society are gay. Gay people are everywhere.

In fact, if we look at the historical record, we marvel at the diversity and achievement of gay people: Socrates and Sappho; Oscar Wilde and Gertrude Stein; Michaelangelo and Gore Vidal; James Baldwin and Tennessee Williams; W.H. Auden and Somerset Maugham. Or, more recently, the courageous announcement of Dave Kopay, a former half-back for the Green Bay Packers, that he, too, is gay. Stereotypes are wrong. Gay people are everywhere.

Or, it occurs to me that we might be able to combat our prejudice against homosexuality by looking carefully at the crime statistics. The major issue in Florida was the charge that gay people are somehow a threat to children in the classroom. Well, quite truthfully, one of my football coaches in high school was much more of a threat to young women than any of my gay teachers were to young men.

Whether we look at the San Francisco police blotters, or whether we look at the FBI statistics, we discover that in proportion to their numbers gay people commit far less crimes than their heterosexual counterparts. In terms of sex crimes, it's far, far less.

In fact, if we are going to hire teachers on the basis of crime statistics, we should first of all hire people who practice chastity; secondly, we should hire homosexuals; and thirdly, we should hire heterosexuals. Which means that both Anita Bryant and I would be among the last to be hired. The myth of homosexual crime is a part of our prejudice.

Or, it occurs to me that we might be able to combat our prejudice against homosexuality through our own experience with a Gay Caucus. Several years ago, in reaction to the oppression of the mainline Protestant, Jewish, and Catholic churches, a few daring individuals created the Metropolitan Community Church, for gay people. While I wish to congratulate the founders, and pay tribute to their courageous pioneering effort, it seems to me to be a shame — a shame that our society has to have a church which segregates people on the basis of their sexuality. My fervent hope and prayer is that in the future we'll no longer need that kind of church — and that all churches will be open to people regardless of their sexual preferences, their nationality, their color, or anything else.

In our own church, for the past two years, we have had a Gay Caucus. It functions not only to give a kind of sanctuary, a sense of community for gay people within our church, (not only to inform, to teach, to educate), but it also exists for those of us who are straight. For in knowing gay people as they sing in the choir, as they serve on our committees, as we wash dishes together in the kitchen, as we come to know them as individual human beings — we are growing — we are learning — we are improving ourselves as people.

That's the importance of our Caucus. I'm proud of it. I wish to honor those who have formed it, and those who have led it, and those who have continued to make it a vital force in our church community.

Or, it also occurs to me that we might be able to combat our prejudice against homosexuality by looking at our own religious tradition. I suppose if I were representing another church tradition I might feel quite differently. But as a Unitarian-Universalist I know that our churches have always been open to people: as early as the 17th Century, open to the Indians; in the period of the Civil War, open to blacks; at the turn of the century, open to waves of immigrants; and the first church in the United States to be open to women in the ministry.

Under the present circumstances, the same principles apply — the two principles — the freedom of the individual and the dignity of each human being. Here are the major ingredients of our religious tradition, which we have an obligation and a duty to express in our lives and in our church. If we understand that heritage, and know that heritage, and appreciate that heritage, we will be open to all of the people who come to our door.

These are some of the ways we might combat our prejudice. But I think to really overcome our deepest feelings, we have to be more than tolerant and patronizing. Personally, I would rather know that a person is an enemy than that a person is a patron. For a patron still has that air of superiority, that air of smugness, which oppressed people never need.

So to really overcome our prejudice, we have to do away with that easy tolerance, and we have to go down to the roots of the lie, and we have to tear it out of our hearts forever. We have to say to ourselves, and to others, the words that Jesus said. He didn't say: "I tolerate you." He said: "I love you," because of who and what you are.

Finally, I remember a memorial service I conducted here in the sanctuary a few years ago. It began when a young man came into my office one afternoon, very disturbed, and told me that his lover had just died. The deceased had been a very prominent member of the San Francisco Gay Community.

The young man asked if I would mind conducting the memorial service. He also said that the parents of his lover were flying in to San Francisco from the East, and that the parents were not informed about their son's gay lifestyle. He couldn't predict how they were going to take it.

Naturally, I was fearful. While I agreed to officiate at the ceremony, I felt that some problem (some horrible embarrassment) was almost certainly going to result. I planned the service — and that evening I walked into the pulpit — and looked out on about 300 people from the gay community — and looked down on the young man who was crying, sitting with the parents of the man who had died.

Immediately, I knew by the expressions on their faces, and by their manner, that everything was fine; that everything was all right — and I sensed throughout the service that love was flowing everywhere. Afterwards, I greeted the parents at the back of the sanctuary and they said to me, "Isn't it nice that our son had so many friends." And I said, "Yes."

I suppose I'm a romantic. I've certainly been charged with being a romantic — I quote from Abelard and Eloise in the pulpit; I love Romeo and Juliet; I still enjoy Clark Gable and Claudette Colbert movies; and I really don't mind the title.

I believe strongly in the family. I believe strongly in marriage. Yes, you can believe strongly in these things and still support homosexuality. There are some things I don't like — prostitution, casual sex, pornography — because I think they are hurtful, destructive, and harmful to the human personality.

But there's one thing a romantic always believes in — and that's love. I believe in love. I don't think anything in our society — oppression, hatred, prejudice — can stand against love. When I witness love between two people: male and female, male and male, female and female — I rejoice! I celebrate that love. I fear nothing where love exists.

And I ask no questions, for love is good, love is God — not even the gates of hell will prevail against it.

Chapter VI

A Day of Feasting And Gladness

"O beautiful for spacious skies,
For amber waves of grain,
For purple mountain majesties
Above the fruited plain!
America! America!
God shed His grace on thee . . ."
— KATHARINE LEE BATES

See America First

I am a dreamer. (Are you a dreamer?)

I have always dreamed of going to Spain! Squeezing wine from a long leather pouch. Swimming in the Mediterranean. Talking to the Anarchists in Barcelona. Visiting the cathedrals in Madrid, and climbing the ancient Pyrenees, and walking through the landscapes of El Greco. But . . . I will probably never get to Spain!

I am a dreamer. (Are you a dreamer?)

I have always dreamed of going to China! Eating Cantonese food in Canton. Praying in the Buddhist temples. Standing on the Great Wall with Genghis Khan. Joining the pilgrims to the Forbidden City, and playing with the children, and writing a poem in Peking. But . . . I will probably never get to China!

I am a dreamer. (Are you a dreamer?)

I have always dreamed of going to Brazil! Walking on the beach at Rio. Listening to the Latin strings and native drums. Sitting with the Indians at noon. Cruising on the Amazon, and looking for Stone Age relics, and hiking through the forests of rare birds and monkeys. But . . . I will probably never get to Brazil!

I know people who have seen the world . . .

> They have climbed the Alps, bathed in the Riviera,
>   kneeled in the Taj Mahal;
> They have danced in Paris, skied in Norway,
>   fished in the Coral Sea;
> They have trekked the jungles of Africa, sailed through
>   the Panama Canal, and wept in Jerusalem.

Yes, I envy those people. For I was nurtured on the books of Richard Halliburton, and I like to scale new mountains, and I am a dreamer. (We are all dreamers!)

131

But since it is not possible to visit the lands of my dreams, I have endeavored to explore the land of my birth. In other words, I have tried to satisfy my wanderlust by following the roads, the paths, and the streams of America. And in the process (to be quite sentimental, I admit) I have fallen in love with the land. Like Stephen Vincent Benet:

> *I have fallen in love with American names,*
> *The sharp gaunt names that never get fat.*
> *The snakeskin-titles of mining claims,*
> *The plumed war-bonnet of Medicine Hat,*
> *Tucson, and Deadwood and Lost Mule Flat.*

Incredible names — an incredible land! It has been an exciting odyssey!

I have walked on the graves of America.

I have kneeled at the monument to the Mayflower voyagers, and at the monument to old Chief Joseph. I have visited the tombs of Lincoln and Jefferson and Adams and Franklin. I have stood on the bones of thousands of soldiers at Fort Necessity, Bunker Hill, Valley Forge, Gettysburg, and Arlington. I have paused at the graves of Wild Bill Hickok, Calamity Jane, Emerson, Robert E. Lee, and Mary Baker Eddy. I have joined the buzzing tourists at the Tomb of the Unknown Soldier, and I have sat alone on the grass at Old Boot Hill. It is good to visit the graves of America. A sobering experience — it brings perspective to the stream of history.

I have enjoyed the beauty of America.

I have climbed the Adirondack Mountains; leaned over the edge of Yellowstone Falls; bathed in two oceans, the Gulf of Mexico, and five Great Lakes. In northern Idaho, there is a lake named Pend Oreille, over two thousand feet deep with the largest trout in the world. In California, you can drive your car through a redwood tree, walk on craters that look like the moon, or visit a desert as hot as the sun. Nebraska has flies as large as birds. Northern New York is Cooperstown, Jamestown, and Watkins Glen. And Texas IS big — Iowa more green than you imagine; there are a thousand lakes in Minnesota — and it is still a thrill to cross the Mississippi.

Stand on the rim of the Snake River Canyon;

Tour the farms in the Blue Grass of Kentucky;

Sink down 600 feet into the caverns at Carlsbad;
And hike the high plateaus of Yosemite.
America, even without Disney, is a wonderland of natural beauty.

I have met the people of America.
I lived with the coalminers of South Fork, Pennsylvania.
I worked with the tough steelmen of Pittsburgh. I attended
college in Amish Country — with horses and buggies and black
suits and bonnets. I chug-a-lugged beer with Slovaks, and Poles,
and Croatians; sipped cocktails with bankers, professors, and
congressmen; and, for some reason, all my barbers have been
Goldwater Republicans.

I sparred with Jersey Joe Walcott, shared tea with Ted Kennedy, and married Red Skelton — that's name dropping!
I was fired by a university president, pursued by the FBI, and
mugged by the best in Boston — that's fear!
And I often recall the panhandler in crowded Times Square
who said: "If you give me a dollar, I promise not to ask
again." That's industry!
It is a land of many contrasts, but nowhere more than in its people
— the richest resource in the richest land.

I have experienced the strangeness of America.
The George Washington Bridge, at rush hour, is a peculiar
kind of hell. Getting hit by a truck in Detroit was almost the
end of the journey, and I was driving a South Bend Studebaker.
Chased wild horses through a Northwest town. Walked in Tom
Sawyer's cave in Hannibal, Missouri. Almost drowned off the
Coronado Beach. My wife bought a hotdog from a Navajo Indian
— and noticed there was nothing inside. Left a prayer at Oral
Roberts' University.

I have walked on a glacier in the Tetons; sailed on the waters
of Buzzard's Bay; and straddled the whole Southwest
at Four Corners.
I have challenged the Truckee rapids; climbed the Washington Monument; and was locked in a cell at Alcatraz.
I have been lost in Cheyenne, Wyoming; confused on the
trails of the Bitterroots; dumbfounded at Columbus
Circle; and scared to death in north Philadelphia.
It is a strange, strange land — with many mysteries, and delights,
and pitfalls. America is infinite variety.

I have been saddened by America.

I have lived in the Appalachian Mountains where the high hills, the streams, and the deep foliage are only a mask for ugliness. Where everything that turns the land into an idyl for the tourist conspires to hold the people down. Where the once proud and independent mountain folk are no longer needed in the mines. Where the people scratch their half-livings from a resistant land. Where poverty and hopelessness are the only reality.

> I have been to Stockton and Fresno where lush farms dominate the countryside. Where thousands of migrant workers live in cheap skid-row hotels and pasteboard shacks. Where a willing mass of human beings sell themselves in the marketplace. Where a mother breastfeeds her infant, and her four-year-old as well, since that will be his only food.

> I have visited Harlem, Houff, and Roxbury — created out of the white man's fear and prejudice. I have seen the Indian lands of Arizona where a lizard feels condemned. I have walked through the boweries of Baltimore, Kansas City, and Seattle, where men hang in doorways and alleys, with no more comfort than a brown paper bag.

> I watched Lake Erie die. I saw the forest burn in Oregon. Sneezed, and choked, and coughed on the fumes of Sandburg's Chicago. Witnessed the skill of tourists, developers, merchants, and mercenaries as they raped and killed the land. Found garbage in the San Bruno hills. East Gary, Indiana is the ugliest place of all.

It is easy to be saddened by America. Not all is good and lovely. There is dirt and pain.

Yet I suggest that before you begin thinking of the castles in Scotland, the beaches in Tahiti, or the small villages of sunny Italy — see America first. If we have littered our parks and seashores; if we have destroyed our historic buildings; if we have polluted our lakes and streams; if we have ignored our old and poor — then let us admit today that we need to renew our love for the land and the people.

See America first! Perhaps a love will be born. Not the jingoistic nationalism that judges the rest of the world. Not the mindless patriotism that ends in acts of aggression. Not the flag-waving nonsense that contributes to pride and ignorance.

But a simple, humble love of country. The kind that says:

> *This is my country. I will cherish what there is to cherish, and I will change what there is to change. It is me – and I am it. Our destiny is with each other.*

SEE AMERICA FIRST . . .

Go to the Lincoln Memorial at midnight . . .

Feel the spray of the water on the rocky coast of Maine . . .

Talk to the Marxist in Atlanta, and the Mormon in Salt Lake, and the Unitarian in Outlaw Ridge . . .

Stop at the Courthouse in Reno — and try to guess who is getting married and who divorced . . .

Mingle with the young people on the Boston Common, Telegraph Avenue, the Village — and really listen to what they say . . .

Visit Harvard, Princeton, and Vassar, Idaho — only a stone's throw from Potlatch . . .

See Old Faithful, Muir Woods in the rain, the Old Man of the Mountain . . .

And don't forget Bourbon Street — the bright lights, the gaiety, the Jazz — the infectious corruption of New Orleans . . .

The St. Lawrence is too cold for swimming; don't leave your car in Death Valley; don't feed the bears in Yellowstone, or walk alone at night in Central Park, or talk too loud in Arkansas . . .

But ride the Edaville Railroad on the Cape; taste the Bing cherries in Washington; sleep in the Painted Desert, and creep through the House of the Seven Gables . . .

Explore America — for there is nothing like it anywhere! America is every height and depth, every length and width, every good and evil, every tongue and color, every love and hatred, every hope and despair — it is everything! It is the largest, boiling meltingpot in the history of the world.

It is worth saving. Curse and complain! Cry out loudly! Clamor for reform! Scream for justice! Build the barricades! But, please, do it all out of love for the land and the people. We must love that which we hope to save — and America is well worth the saving.

In the words of Woody Guthrie, who spoke for the migrants (and all of us are migrants):

It's a mighty hard row that my pore hands have hoed,
My pore feet have traveled a hot dusty road,
Out of your dustbowl and westward we rolled,
Your deserts was hot and your mountains was cold.

Green pastures of plenty from dry desert ground,
From the Grand Coulee Dam where the water runs down,
Every state in this union us migrants have been,
And we'll work in this fight and we'll fight 'til we win.

Oh, its always we rambled, your river and I,
All along your green valley I'll work 'til I die,
My land I'll defend with my life need it be,
Green pastures of plenty must always be free!

"Between the finite limitations of the five senses
and the endless yearnings of man for the beyond
the people hold to the humdrum bidding of work and food
while reaching out when it comes their way
for lights beyond the prism of the five senses,
for keepsakes lasting beyond any hunger or death."
— CARL SANDBURG

The Miracles of Easter

The Fighter

I remember a young man who wanted to be a professional fighter. He was tall and thin for a middleweight, but he possessed a hard head, better than average speed, and a good right hand. Besides, he had grown up in a neighborhood where fighting was the only mark of distinction, and he looked forward to a successful career.

In fact, he was rather conceited about his own ability. He had been coached at the YMCA; he had never suffered a loss; and he had been described as a natural fighter. So though his head was hard, it was infinitely inflatable, and he succumbed to a sense of self-importance that would have embarrassed Napoleon himself.

It was in the semi-finals of a local tournament that the young warrior met his Waterloo. His opponent was shorter, heavier, thicker — but did not appear to have the speed or experience to beat the next champion of the world. They sparred carefully during the first round, with the young man easily out-scoring the shorter fighter. Naturally, he was extremely confident.

In the second round, he saw an opening that signalled the end. He jabbed hard with the left hand, and crashed his opponent into the ropes with a strong right cross. With the shorter fighter no longer able to defend, the young man set him up with two lefts to the chin, a right hook to the head, another left to the midsection, and finally, the hardest right cross he had ever delivered. He then stepped back to survey the destruction.

Imagine his surprise when his opponent did not fall! Imagine his dismay when his opponent showed no pain, no blood, no glaze in the eyes! Imagine his unutterable shock when his opponent

137

simply looked, then smiled, and then laughed at the feeble effort of the thin young man! The fight would end in the third round, but the smile was the real end. It was the end of a fight — the end of a dream — and the end of a career.

Of course . . . the young man went on to become a Unitarian minister in San Francisco, California. He is now quite older, certainly slower, and a little more humble. He is even able to look back on that smile as the first step in a Resurrection scene — the first step of growth and maturity — that would lead to a more fruitful life.

"Thanks," he is sometimes heard to say, "I needed that!"

The Mother

I remember a woman in New Bedford, Massachusetts. Middle-aged, attractive, and with no formal education — her life had been marred by a series of tragedies.

As the daughter of a poor fisherman, she had known hard times.

As the bride of an older man, she had been unhappy in marriage.

As a divorced woman in a Catholic community, she had known many humiliations.

But the crowning tragedy occurred when her teenage son was found by the police. He was unconscious, surrounded by drugs and needles. At the hospital, it was determined that he had suffered an overdose of heroin. He died shortly thereafter, with newspaper headlines adding to the grief.

When I first met the mother, I noticed an air of unreality, an inability to deal with the terrible loss. She said her son had been suffering from a severe illness. She said the police had often harassed the family. In her mind she was trying to sort out all of the factors that might have led to the death of her son. It was the reaction of a thoroughly crushed and drained individual.

But a few weeks later, she quietly entered my office and calmly inquired: "Do you suppose I could use a room in the church for a meeting next week? I would like to invite the mothers of some drug addicts for a discussion." Surprised by her request, but impressed by her manner, I immediately complied.

Well . . . the end of the story is in the form of an Easter miracle.

The first meeting attracted three mothers, over coffee and
   doughnuts.
The second meeting attracted many mothers and fathers,
   who openly discussed their children's addiction.
And future meetings attracted parents, reporters, and public
   officials for the first sessions ever held on the problem
   of drug addiction.
In the months to follow, the original organizer was a dynamo
of energy:
   She spoke to the Board of Trustees — and the basement of
      the church was converted into a Drug Rehabilitation
      Center.
   She spoke to the Mental Health officials — and the city
      established a Drug Prevention Unit for the people of
      the community.
   She spoke to the State and Federal agencies — and New
      Bedford was able to create one of the most effective
      drug programs in the nation.
Indeed, the last I heard, she was still organizing, lecturing, and
traveling all over New England — wherever an addict could be
found. Out of the tears, out of the ashes, out of the cave of grief
and mourning — a new life, with a new purpose, had emerged.
The stone had been rolled away!

The Child
   I remember driving along a narrow country road in northern
New York. It was upper-Appalachia: where the rocky soil could
no longer support the crops; where local industry had been abandoned to the wind and cold; and where over sixty per cent of the
people were existing on welfare. I had never seen an area so devoid
of joy and hope — not even in the slums and ghettos of the largest
cities.
   Earlier, Ginger and I had spoken to a social worker about the
possibility of adopting a child. We were not optimistic, since we
had no money, no home, no references, and two more years of
Graduate School before I could find employment. But after six
years of marriage — we knew that we wanted a child.
   Much to our surprise, the social worker encouraged our
application. She explained that because of the grinding poverty
in the area, there were many children living on the farms and

in the foster homes who were eligible for adoption. In fact, the oversupply was quite critical, with not nearly enough people applying for the available children.

So we were driving along the narrow road to the County Welfare building, a large stone mansion in the middle of a desolate field. It was only eight weeks after our initial interview, but we were going to be introduced to a 22-month-old child named Mark. I was talking more than usual. Ginger was talking less than usual. We were both excited!

When we arrived, we were taken up two flights of old wooden stairs into a large room — half office and half playground. Sitting on the floor, in the far corner, was a little boy with his back to the intruders. With round sloping shoulders, uncombed strawberry hair, an incredibly chubby face, and dimples in his elbows, he was the model of a Michelangelo angel.

We talked together — he knew many words.

We played together — he rolled a rubber ball.

We cried together — Mark, and Ginger, and myself.

And as long as I live on this earth, I will never forget the joy of that moment. For we had found a son! Three whole lives had been suddenly and dramatically changed! It was truly a time to rejoice. It was Easter in Appalachia!

The Wedding

> It was not the wedding of two young people
> who have their whole lives before them.
> It was not the large church wedding with pretty
> gowns, and flowers, and the sound of organ.
> It was not the small home wedding with friends
> and relatives celebrating the event.
> Nonetheless — it was a most memorable wedding!

The groom was a short-order cook, who had been a drifter all his life, working in carnivals, cafes, bus terminals, truck stops, and moving from town to town as the season dictated. He was about sixty years old; quiet, kind, and extremely lonely.

The bride was a member of my church, who worked as a secretary in a local factory. She was shy and unassuming, seldom noticeable in a crowd of people, preferring an inward and private existence. She was about fifty years old; quiet, kind, and extremely lonely.

The wedding was performed in the late afternoon of Christmas Eve. The groom was dressed in a dark blue suit, with a white shirt, and a terrible blue tie. The bride was attired in a long white gown, with no discernible make-up, and red bathrobe tied at the waist. For you see, we were gathered together at the hospital — and the bride was terminally ill.

Yet, as I read the words of the Wedding Ceremony, all that was forgotten. The groom appeared so strong and loving that I was reminded of Romeo, Abelard, and Prince Valiant all wonderfully mixed together. The bride appeared so brave and radiant that I was reminded of Juliet, Eloise, and Sleeping Beauty all wonderfully mixed together. Even the noise in the hall seemed to stop, and the bells seemed to ring, as the ceremony concluded with a kiss.

As I departed from the room, they were hugging and laughing on the edge of the bed. If they had only a night together, or a week, or a month — it would be more than they had ever dreamed. I wished them both a Merry Christmas! Yet I knew in my heart what I had witnessed. It was not the impulsive pleasure of Christmas, but the inexplicable joy of Easter!

The Meaning of Easter

What we want to learn from religion is how we might become new and better men and women, boys and girls.

How can we conquer our evil passions?

How can we master our faults and weaknesses?

How can we lay hold of joy and genuine happiness?

How can we attain the significant and the eternal?

In other words, how can we improve the quality of our lives in the days and years remaining?

The traditional Easter Story is a reminder that such renewal is possible.

It is a reminder that life is essentially timeless and spiritual. We are not bound to the past.

It is a reminder that life is not simply a collection of events, but a quest for ideals. We are not bound to the present.

It is a reminder that life is not only decay and destruction, but also birth and creation. We are not bound to a particular future.

It was this promise of renewal that Jesus brought to his disciples.

"Verily, verily, I say unto you, that ye shall weep and lament, but the world shall rejoice . . . and ye shall be sorrowful, but your sorrow shall be turned into joy."

Yet Easter is more than an ancient story. It is many modern stories. It is a real and ever-present possibility for everyone:

> If we open our minds to new channels of thought and learning;
>
> If we open our hearts to new modes of loving and living;
>
> If we open our eyes to new models of growth and significance —

Easter will appear! It will supply us with courage. It will take us on great adventures. It will save us from pride, grief, and apathy. It will bind us to joy and to hope again!

A Sort of Christmas Story

I knew an old woman once.

Several years ago, I was a student studying for the ministry at St. Lawrence Theological School. Each morning, I drove the eleven miles from Hermon to Canton in rural New York, and each evening I returned. It was not an uneventful journey.

In time, I came to know not just the twists and turns of the road, but the bend of the trees, the rocks in the stream, the farm animals, the children waiting for their yellow bus, and a wide variety of sounds, and sights, and smells.

The truth is that I actually looked forward to the journey: waving at the elderly teacher as she passed on her way to work; waiting for the German shepherd to chase my wheels as the car pulled over a rise in the road; watching for the derelict who walked the gutters in search of discarded bottles; and passing a one-room shack along the way where an old woman made her home.

In the Fall, the old woman chopped wood in preparation for Winter. She boarded up the broken windows, stuffed the crack in the door with paper; and some mornings, her work completed, she sat on the stoop reading a day-old paper, or a month-old, or a year-old — it really didn't matter.

Occasionally, in the evening, I saw the old woman, in her tattered dress and tennis shoes, finishing the chores for the day. But more often, especially in the winter months, she retreated to the shack where the kerosene lamp flickered in the window, and the wood stove pushed black smoke into the chill night air.

Day after day, and night after night, I observed that shack and that old woman. I asked about her in the town — but no one

143

knew too much. The mailman delivered food. She had no family, no friends, no visitors. She never talked to anyone. She liked to be alone.

Often, I would think of stopping to put money in the mailbox that stood along the road. On reflection, I decided that such an act of charity would somehow violate her sense of pride and independence. So, I merely waved and smiled — and even at times pretended to ignore her — so as not to make her feel like an object of curiosity.

But soon, I was able to witness a strange transformation. In the mornings, she seemed to be inching closer and closer to the road, as if waiting for the car. And in the evenings (even in the coldest weather) she would stand by the window, as if wanting to be seen.

Then, one day, she waved . . . she waved! It was not much of a wave — no expression on the face, the arm half-lifted, the hand barely moving. But it was a wave. Perhaps her first, ever. I don't know. An old woman, one-hundred years old (I later learned), waving to a student on his way to school.

Then, one morning, after not seeing her for several days, I stopped the car, walked to the partially open door, and peeked inside. It was empty and cold, with garbage and newspapers scattered on the floor. On the door was a note, written in a nervous scribble. It read: "To mailman. Tell young man — gone for the day." And so she was. For she had died.

> *Lady of silences*
> *Calm and distressed*
> *Torn and most whole*
> *Rose of memory*
> *Rose of forgetfulness . . .*
> *The silent sister veiled in white and blue*
> *Between the trees, behind the garden god,*
> *Whose flute is breathless,*
> *Bent her head, and sighed, but spoke no word . . .*
> *But you are the music – while the music lasts.*

Merry Christmas!

Chapter VII

And He Shall Perform All My Pleasure

> "Do not be frightened, old man. What is
> the matter? Come on, quiet down. They are
> only killing Judas, silly."
> — JUAN JIMENEZ

My Name Is Judas Iscariot

*(Scene: It is Good Friday. The speaker is standing in the middle
of a bare chancel. The only lights are on him as he begins.)*

My name is Judas — Judas Iscariot.

I am an early member of that small company of betrayers
whose names have become part of the language of infamy. No one
has been hated by more people, for so long, and with so much
passion.

I have been murdered again, and again, and again. No one
claims me. No one defends me. Would you take just a moment
to listen to my story? It is the season for stories.

My parents were fine people, well-educated, and deeply
religious. My father was a merchant by trade — proud and fiercely
independent by nature. He was also very brave, and after joining
in one of the local uprisings against Roman rule in Israel, he
was arrested and imprisoned. The Romans crucified my father.
My mother's spirit died with him.

I was adrift for the next few years. I wandered aimlessly
around the countryside, thinking only of how to avenge my
father's death. I was overwhelmed by a deep hatred of the Romans
— their laws, their legions, their puppet rulers — and I prayed
for their destruction.

In time, I joined a small band of Zealots in the hill country
of Galilee. Our purpose was to establish an underground movement as the spearhead of a popular uprising. But there were too
many Romans, and we were not accepted by the people, and
all seemed lost!

Then, as if in answer to my prayer, through the small villages
of Galilee came the prophet, Jesus of Nazareth. Most of the people
thought of him as merely the son of a poor carpenter, deranged,
perhaps, and certainly inviting death with his talk of a "New
Kingdom." They laughed at his teachings — for they knew his
family.

My feelings were different. I saw the miracles. I felt the inner power and strength of the prophet. When he spoke of the new age to come I was lifted up as never before. My spirits soared! My hopes revived! For here was the heir of David. Here was the Messiah of Israel. Here was the King so long awaited. Or so I wished to believe.

After speaking with Jesus, it was decided that I could join the disciples — the last of the twelve chosen for the inner circle of leadership. Although the youngest of the group, my background proved valuable, for I was immediately selected as Keeper of the Purse — a difficult task in those days of poverty.

While I was often criticized for a quick temper and impatience, it should be noted that I gained the title of "Apostle," and I performed miracles and cast out demons as well as the others. Many thought I was the favorite of the Master. Even Peter was sometimes jealous!

I was impatient. Often, around the fire at night, or along the lonely dusty roads, I would ask Jesus about the coming Kingdom: when would it finally arrive; what kind of rule would he establish; what role would I play in the scheme? But he did not commit himself.

I was confused. He spoke for the law and against the law; for the Temple and against the Temple; for the Romans and against the Romans. At times he spoke only in riddles, in parables that none of us, his closest companions, could understand. It was maddening!

Until one day — one day he announced in solemn tones that we were going to Jerusalem. It was then that I cast away all doubts and knew that the time had come. For Jerusalem was the seat of Roman power — the target for the true Messiah!

All during the week of Passover I was anxious for victory. We marched through the gates of the city with a large procession. The crowds of pilgrims shouted: "Hosanna in the highest!" — and greeted Jesus as the Son of David.

The following day, hundreds of our people pressed into the Temple area, overturning the tables of the money-changers, driving out the merchants, and challenging the authority of the priests. In the courtyard, Jesus cursed the rulers and spoke to the multitudes, while I stood with him, expectantly, knowing that all of Jerusalem could be ours before the day was ended.

And then . . . and then . . . he fled! At dawn of the next day, when the first of the soldiers approached the Temple, Jesus counselled our people to retreat. While many remained to resist the legions, they were quickly subdued. Our "leader" escaped in the confusion. He ran from the city. He went up into the hills to hide, like a child running from the dogs.

Now listen! . . . I want you to understand . . . I will not be long. I want you to understand that I was filled with shame and disgust. All my plans — all my hopes — all my dreams — all the promises — everything was crushed!

My despair increased when the urchins of the streets laughed and jeered at the flight of the so-called "Savior of the Jews." When I was first questioned by the Temple guards, I spit in their faces and refused to speak; but later, I hinted that I might help them. After all, it was over. It was finished. Who had really been betrayed?

I quickly made my way to the hideout in the hills near Bethany. One by one the disciples appeared, hoping to learn of future plans, or at least the reason for the recent failure. But there was little talking — and no explanation. All were weary and afraid.

That evening, as we were eating in an upper room, Jesus said: "One of you will betray me." When the others questioned him as to whom it would be, he said to them: "It is one of the twelve," and it seemed he was looking at me. I did not reply.

After the meal, I waited until Jesus went into the garden on the slope of the Mount of Olives, and then I hurried down across the river to the home of a priest. I announced my plan and I was provided with the necessary guard.

While Jesus was still praying, I approached in the company of soldiers and called out: "Rabbi! Rabbi!" — and when he appeared from the darkness, I embraced and kissed him. The soldiers took him easily.

Even then, you see, if he had been the Anointed One, the Son of David, the King of Kings, he could have called down the wrath of God upon his captors! Yet he did nothing. They led him away for trial — and crucifixion.

So you can judge the distortion of history. I have been condemned by those who never understood my motives, and slandered by those who are blind to truth. It has been claimed that I betrayed Jesus for a small reward, but I had no foolish desire for a few pieces of silver! I was not in pursuit of fame or fortune! NO! I wanted only what had been promised — and what small justice this world affords.

Truth? What is truth?

I believed that Jesus was a false Messiah; a false prophet, erring and making to err; a beguiler and one who led astray; one whom the Law commanded to be killed; and one to whom God forbade pity, or compassion, or forgiveness. Further, I believed that his sin was the worst kind of atrocity. He raised false hopes in the hearts of those who worshipped him.

Truth? What is truth?

I can only say, in truth, that no one loved him as I loved him — and for that reason, no one could hate him half as much. Is that not the truth?

After the death of Jesus, my depression increased. The Rabbi's followers turned to the synagogues and became increasingly subservient to Rome, upon whom they depended for their existence. The radical Jewish element had lost its heart — as old guard Zealots were either dead or in hiding. The hired puppets of the Romans were in complete control of Israel.

I had no future . . . I destroyed myself.

Was it an act of repentance, as my enemies have claimed? No. I had lost all faith in Jesus! Look at his behavior before the judges, before the accusers, and all manner of contempt and scorn. Look at his behavior on the cross.

He did not resist . . .

He did not defend his right . . .

He took no step to ward off the end . . .

On the contrary, he provoked it, and almost seemed to welcome it, as if death itself were victory.

I would remind you that he came to send fire on the earth — in his own words — "not to bring peace but a sword." Yet he refused the instrument of violence; he walked meekly to his death; and he forgave the very soldiers who pierced his flesh. Was he a savior? Or a weak and deluded man? Was I to blame? Or did he bring it on himself? I only know — I had no sense of guilt.

He was kind. I have no desire for total condemnation. His love and compassion for the poor was honest and touching. His mild manner and gentle speech softened the hardest of men. Pity, patience, intelligence were among his many virtues. And the good he accomplished lived after him in the minds and hearts of the other disciples. It cannot be taken from his legacy.

But my God, my God, where was the Kingdom? Where was the new Empire announced by the prophets of old? Where was the heavenly Savior, described by Isaiah: "Who brings princes to nought, and makes the rulers of the earth as nothing"?

Oh, we had waited so long! I wanted to see, and feel, and hear, and smell. I wanted judgment. I wanted power. I wanted justice. Not meekness, humility, surrender — but strength, courage, and victory. Not a miserable symbol on a cross — but an indestructible King! Is that so difficult to understand? Not to justify! Or even to forgive! But to understand?

Why do you hate me?

It is not because of the betrayal of Jesus. For without Good Friday, there would have been no Easter — and Christianity would have died in the hills of Bethany.

Why do you hate me?

It is not because I am morally inferior to Christians. For the Church, in the name of Jesus, has engaged in persecutions, crusades, inquisitions — none of which I condoned.

Why do you hate me?

It is not because your own generation is pure. For the Twentieth Century is the greatest witness to the principles of violence and warfare that the world has ever known — and I never sanctioned that brutality.

Then, why do you hate me?

Is it not because you need to hate? Is it not because you need to have a Judas Tree, and a Judas Goat, and a Judas Neighbor, and a Judas People in order to justify yourselves? Am I not only the symbol of your own suppressed fear and insecurity? Is not that the truth?

I am only a man. A frail man. Mistaken, perhaps. Perhaps not. But you have murdered me — again, and again, and again. My dying is delightful to your eyes.

Yes — you are killing Judas — the betrayer.

But you are also killing those whom you only label as Judas — a convenient excuse.

And most of all — you are killing a part of yourselves, for there is a little of Judas in everyone.

In everyone.

(EXIT)

"if there is a god
i think he must be shaped something like a mountain
and something like a tree
and something like an ocean ...
i imagine he looks something like a black man
and something like a white man
and something like a yellow man
and something like a woman, too ..."
— J. DAVID SCHEYER

Oglethorpe P. Bushmaster of Punxsatawney, Pennsylvania

In the capacity of counselor, I meet people every day who are severely crippled by adversity. It is sometimes true that they have experienced a terrible loss or a horrible pain, but it is also true that they have abandoned all perspective on the human condition, while sinking into a pattern of remorse and self-pity.

The world is nothing but a vast conspiracy against them.

The misfortune of others is nothing in comparison to their own.

The future is nothing but a dull repetition of the past.

So they curse the gods, or damn their fate, or bitterly complain — with no appreciation of their own creativity, or their own beauty, or their own magnificence as human beings.

Yet I have known other people, who have experienced a mountain of adversity, with no apparent effect on their ability to function as healthy members of society. They are equally difficult to understand.

Their world is a series of disasters.

Their misfortune is a daily reality.

Their future is marked with uncertainty.

But they are able to develop a unique perspective; and they are able to depend on a host of resources; and they are able to mold a constructive life out of the very adversity that afflicts them. Not only Jesus, or Buddha, or Gandhi — the gifted saints of history — but the most devilish people as well.

His name was Oglethorpe P. Bushmaster. Or was it Charles Bogle? Or Cuthbert J. Twillie? Or was it Mahatma Kane Jeeves?

While it was often difficult to trap him into telling the truth about anything, he was born William Claude Dukinfield on April 9, 1879. He successfully defied civilization for sixty-seven years, and he is toasted as one of the beloved kings of American comedy. When I have problems, I often think of him.

His father was a London cockney who had settled in the Germantown district of Philadelphia as a fruit and vegetable salesman. He was prey to fits of tyranny. His mother was a hard-working housewife with an exceptional measure of native shrewdness. She was an unpopular mimic of the neighborhood. The son would later say that both his father and his mother had suffered from leprosy — a blatant falsehood! Yet William was dangerously bored by the time he was four, and greatly preferred a life of fantasy.

As a child, he was sensitive, mulish, humorous, and independent.

At the age of five, he worked with his father on the cart, falsely publicizing vegetables like "rutabagas, pomegranates, and calabashes," simply because the names pleased him. The father beat him daily.

At the age of six, he entered school one Monday in the autumn of the year, and managed to stay until almost noon, at which time his formal education was concluded. The teacher was greatly relieved.

At the age of eleven, he took a large wooden box to the hayloft in the stable, and when his father entered, he dropped it on his head. He walked off down the road and never returned. The family made little more than a token search.

For the next three years, William was a one-child crime wave. He lived in a barrel, a barn, a cellar, a saloon, and almost every jail in Philadelphia. It is believed that he committed every misdemeanor and small felony in the Criminal Code. Indeed, he was looked upon by the police as a corrupting influence on the older inmates, and he was usually released on the unspoken grounds that he would utterly destroy the prison system.

Yet the man, later to be known as W.C. Fields, could easily be seen in the child.

In order to distinguish himself, he developed a grandiose air, shot through with fraud, that stuck with him like plaster for the rest of his life. It would later be evidenced in the cutaway coat, morning trousers, and a tall silk hat.

Due to the constant exposure to the elements, his voice cracked, hoarsened, mellowed and reformed on a note of permanent rasp. It would later result in a nasal mutter, greatly imitated by everyone.

And as a result of many beatings, his nose was reduced to a pulp so often that, in gaining scar tissue, it rapidly added dimension. It would later dominate the face like an Idaho potato.

So, in the midst of crime, poverty, and animal survival, a national character was beginning to take shape — a rare institution of absurdity and humor.

He worked for a time as a newsboy, an ice-boy, and a pool hustler — but his real passion was the ancient art of juggling, which he had first seen in a traveling circus. He would later write:

> I still carry scars on my legs from those early attempts at juggling. I'd balance a stick on my toe, toss it into the air, and try to catch it again on my toe. Hour after hour the damned thing would bang against my shinbones. I'd work until tears were streaming down my face. But I kept on practicing, and bleeding, until I perfected the trick.

For a child of thirteen, it was a demonstration of tremendous will power, and it marked an inner compulsion that would never bow to adversity. When the times were most difficult, he simply worked harder — until his hands were raw and his body wracked with pain.

It would be hard to exaggerate the wretchedness of Field's life in this period. Early photographs of the young juggler reveal him as almost handsome, with a full head of light-colored hair parted near the middle; a firm, self-contained, indomitable line of a mouth; and humorous, quizzical eyes. In the rest of his face was written the hard score of his fight for survival, as he tramped to the booking offices, starved, froze, and became so threadbare he was ashamed to be seen in public.

But he could juggle! With stolen tennis balls, hats, sticks, cigar boxes, and other assorted junk, he carried the art to heights previously unknown — while mixing comedy with athletic skill.

At an amusement park in Norristown, Pennsylvania, for twenty-five cents a day. He stole everything in sight.

At a pier in Atlantic City for fifty cents a day. He doubled as a dummy for the lifeguards to rescue.

With a carnival in the Midwest for $10 a week. He described
    St. Louis as "the igloo of the theatrical world."
In vaudeville for $125 a week. He was known as "W.C.
    Fields: Distinguished Comedian" — at his own request.
On a world tour for $25,000 a year. He later claimed to have
    a thousand illegitimate children in convenient parts of
    the world.
And in the Ziegfield Follies for $50,000 a year. He shared top
    billing with Fanny Brice, Will Rogers, and Eddie Cantor.
By the year 1931, W.C. Fields was not only the best known juggler
in the world, but also an acclaimed dramatic actor on Broadway,
a great comic artist in the film industry, and one of the richest
men in America.

The transition from juggling to comedy was a natural
progression. For the image of Fields on the screen was little
different from the Fields of flesh and blood. While the audiences
were delighted at his portrayal of the fast-talking fraud, the
pompous skinflint, the cheating golfer, the angry individualist,
and the suspicious citizen, they never realized they were laughing
at Fields himself.

Charlie Chaplin was not really "The Tramp."
Buster Keaton was not really "The Country Boy."
But W.C. Fields was always "W.C. Fields."

Rarely has fact and fiction been so artfully blended, as a lifetime
of tragedy merged into a popular comedy on the silver screen.
In his private life, he had developed a phobia about poverty.
Worried about losing his money, or being stranded in a strange
town, he would open a bank account everywhere he went.
Sometimes he hopped off trains and opened an account while an
engine took on water. At one time he had over seven hundred
accounts in banks all over the world. Since he never kept records,
and always used an assumed name, much of his wealth was
never recovered.

In his private life, he had developed an addiction to alcohol.
It began with a few beers to calm him down. It led to carrying
three wardrobe trunks on his travels, one for his clothes and
equipment, and two for his gin and vermouth. It led still further
to a two quart consumption of gin every day — not counting rum,
wine, and brandy — which Fields refused to classify as alcohol.
It was the source of many of his best one-liners:

"I never drink anything stronger than gin before breakfast," he said.

"I don't believe in dining on an empty stomach," he said.

"Who took the cork out of my dinner?" he said.

But he suffered the varied illnesses of alcoholic addiction for many years — and died of a diseased liver in 1946.

In his private life, he had developed a pattern of retreat and isolation, which made him suspicious of all his neighbors, opposed to all forms of government, and loathing animals as reincarnations of old enemies.

He did live with a number of women in the early years of his career.

He did enter into a brief marriage from which a son was born.

And he did have a few close friends in the Hollywood colony whom he loved and respected.

But Fields was never comfortable in society. Despising celebrities, and thumbing his nose at convention, he is best remembered as one of the loneliest of people. It never seemed to bother him.

I have many favorite memories of Fields. I think of him when he first arrived in Hollywood, and walked into the most exclusive hotel he could find. At the desk, he rapped with his cane and asked for "the bridal suite." When the manager informed him that the bridal suite was reserved for gentlemen with brides, Fields replied, "I'll pick one up in town."

Or I think of him on the movie set with Baby Leroy, when the action was suspended so that the infant could have his orange juice. Unseen, Fields had strengthened the citrus with a generous measure of gin. When the child was brought before the camera, the director complained of his lack of animation. Despite the most urgent attempts to revive him, he remained glassy-eyed and in a partial coma. "He's no trouper," Fields kept yelling. "The kid's no trouper. Send him home!"

Or I think of him filling out his income tax forms, and including things like depreciation on vaudeville houses where he had played, salaries for ball rackers, and donations to churches in the Solomon Islands.

Or I think of him frantically chasing a swan around his private lake in Beverly Hills, first with a cane, then with a number four iron, and finally with a loaded revolver — until bitten in the rear.

> Or I think of him, onstage by himself, leaning against a huge piece of scenery, which fell forward with a dusty "thwack" at his feet. "They don't build these houses the way they used to," he roared, as the audience broke up with laughter.

Or I am reminded of the fact that he loved to cultivate flowers. Or I am amazed at the fact that no one ever saw him drunk. Or I am surprised by the fact that he never appreciated locker-room humor. Or I am impressed by the fact that he willed his fortune to destitute children.

By far the best analysis of Fields comes from his closest friend, Gregory La Cava. He believed that Fields' personal and professional life was dedicated to repaying society for the hurts of his childhood. "Nearly everything Bill tried to get into his movies was something that lashed out at the world," he wrote. "The peculiar thing is — that although he was being pretty mean — there wasn't any real sting in it. It was only funny. Bill never really wanted to hurt anybody. He just felt an obligation."

But if I had to select a single scene out of the life of William Claude Dukinfield that best explains his survival as a functioning human being, it would not be one of humor or of tragedy. Rather, I would think of him in the early years of struggle, as he traveled from town to town in tattered clothes. I would think of him in a small hotel, as he stood beside his bed tossing objects into the air. And I would think of him sleeping through the lonely night — all bruised, and cut, and bleeding — as he made ready for the challenge of tomorrow. It is a remarkable scene of courage and dedication.

So the life of W.C. Fields is a striking endorsement of Shakespeare's thoughtful phrase: "Sweet are the uses of adversity." For the misfortune of childhood seemed to play a vital role in his later success. It summoned forth a personal discipline, an iron will, and a spirit of self-sacrifice that would not have been revealed under other circumstances. Instead of stunting, crippling, or defeating him — it induced a savage response.

Finally, it should be obvious that Fields never claimed a formal religion. In general, he felt that the average minister should be unfrocked immediately and prevented, by force if necessary, from communicating any ideas to persons under thirty-five. Yet, in a strange way, his own life was a powerful parable. It says:

We are all born without our consent;
We are all poor victims of the world;
Yet we need not be crushed by anything.
For we each have a skill or a passion;
We each have a gift for the world;
And we need only courage to prevail.

If it is not the Sermon on the Mount, or the Eight-Fold Path, or the Wisdom of Confucius, it is at least a healthy admonition.
To those who are thrown by adversity —
To those who persist in self-pity —
To those who fail to appreciate themselves.

"Godfrey Daniel! Mother of Pearl!" — every life has meaning.

> "Sweet are the uses of adversity;
> Which, like the toad, ugly and venomous,
> Wears yet a precious jewel in his head;
> And this our life, exempt from public haunt,
> Finds tongues in trees, books in the running
> brooks, sermons in stones — and good in
> everything."
> — WILLIAM SHAKESPEARE

I Remember Papa

(Scene: St. Peter is standing behind a high lectern facing the congregation. The woman is behind a smaller lectern with her back to the congregation. No one can see her face.)

St. Peter: Good morning!

Daughter: Hello.

St. Peter: I understand that you are present today to speak on behalf of your father. Is that correct?

Daughter: Yes, it is. But I'm afraid I won't be heard. The other witnesses have been so numerous. Is it possible that I could save him?

St. Peter: My dear young lady, it is not my function to save or condemn! I merely take the testimony. I keep the records on everyone who ever lived on earth, but I do not judge them. That is for a higher power.

Daughter: Then where should I begin? I have so many memories of my father. His life was long and varied. Where should I begin?

St. Peter: "In my beginning is my end," said the poet, "and in my end is my beginning." So it does not matter! Do not be alarmed — and speak only what is in your heart. When did you see him last?

Daughter: In the hospital. He was lying unconscious. The stroke had been severe. He'd lost his speech, and his right side was paralyzed. He opened his eyes several times, but no one knew whether he could see or not.

St. Peter: What did you do? Speak slowly now. I must not miss a word.

Daughter: I was sitting at his side holding his hand, and he looked at me — though I'm sure he couldn't see me. I kissed his face. There was nothing more for me to do . . .

St. Peter: If our hours were all serene, we might probably take almost as little note of them as the clock does of those that are clouded. Yet the death of a parent is a terrible shock, and I am sorry. Please go on! What were you feeling about your father at the time?

Daughter: It's a strange thing, but during those days of illness, when he was nothing but a body out of which the soul had flown, I loved my father more tenderly than I ever had before.

St. Peter: It is not uncommon . . .

Daughter: He'd been remote from me, from us, his children — and all his relatives. Yet, even the grandchildren, who never saw him, loved him . . . and love him still. During those days, when he found peace at last on his death bed and his face became beautiful and serene, I felt my heart breaking from grief and love.

St. Peter: The ultimate goal of life is to know that we are loved. I am sure your father knew of your affection.

As for grief: people bring us miserable consolation when they tell what time will do to help our grief. For our grief is bound up with our love — and we could not cease to mourn without being robbed of our affection.

Are you able to continue?

Daughter: Yes . . . Are you recording everything?

St. Peter: O yes! I have it all. Go on!

Daughter: I felt such a powerful welling-up of strong contra-dictory emotions. I stared at his beautiful face, in its sadness and repose; and listened to the strains of the funeral music; and remembered so many of the events of the past . . .

I thought what a bad daughter I had been; that I'd been more like a stranger than a daughter; and had never been a help to this lonely spirit, this sick old man, when he was in need of family and friends.

St. Peter: Such thoughts are common to the living, who can do no more for the dead. There is always the anguish of guilt — but it, too, will pass.

Daughter: Yet he was, after all, my father! A father who had done his best to love me, and to whom I owed good things as well as bad . . .

All those days I couldn't cry and I didn't eat. A sort of calm had turned me to stone. . . .

St. Peter: It has been said that "we are so largely the plaything of our fears." To one, fear of the dark. To another, of physical pain. To a third, of public ridicule. To a fourth, of poverty. To a fifth, of loneliness. For all of us — our own particular creature lurks in ambush. Nor is it our choice of place or creature. . . .

Believe me, I know better than most your feeling. I, too, once turned to stone, and abandoned a dying friend. It was the one great shame of my life. A bitter . . . well . . . go on!

Daughter: Finally, he died. Many people came in and went silently to the bed to weep. All of them were sincere. No one was merely acting out of loyalty or making a show of their grief. They knew that I had been a bad daughter and that my father had been a bad father — but that he loved me all the same, as I loved him.

St. Peter: It appears that he was a man of some reputation — a celebrity perhaps!

Daughter: Yet no friend ever thought of him as a God or Superman. He was loved and respected, not for his great achievements, but for the most ordinary human qualities: those qualities of which friends are the best judges of all.

St. Peter: Yes, I know! The best mirror is an old friend. But what about the early years? Do you remember your father when you were a little girl? Are there any memories you would like to record? They might be helpful to his case!

Daughter: I remember the early years. We lived on a farm in the country. What I liked was the wonderful garden and terraces on every side of the house. The garden, the flowers, and the woods were my father's hobby and relaxation.

St. Peter: Then he was close to the earth. A farmer perhaps?

Daughter: Well, he never dug in the earth or took a shovel in his hands the way real farmers do, but he liked things to be cultivated. He liked to see cherries, apples, and tomatoes — everywhere!

St. Peter: One could do worse than to be a gardener. I was a humble fisherman.

Daughter: He would spend hours walking in the garden as if he were seeking a quiet, comfortable spot and not able to find it. But this was all the luxury he ever wanted. It showed his healthy appetite for life — his enduring love of the earth.

St. Peter: Your father was a man of simple tastes?

Daughter: Yes. He lived on the ground floor of the old house. He lived in one room, in fact, and made it do for everything. He slept on the sofa. A great soft rug and a fireplace were all the comforts he allowed. Yes. He was a man of simple tastes.

St. Peter: What do you remember most about your father when you were a child? Is there any particular memory?

Daughter: He was away most of the time.

My father's letters were always welcome! They were all written, with great effort, in huge block letters. They always ended: "I kiss you." . . . I was quite small when he wrote this one — (I think I have it here) . . . Yes . . .

"You don't write to your little papa. I think you've forgotten him. How is your health? You're not sick are you? How are your dolls? I thought I'd be getting an order from you soon, but no, too bad, Never mind. I kiss you. I am waiting to hear from you."

Signed — your Little Papa

St. Peter: If I may, I would like to keep that for the records. It is an excellent piece of evidence. Everything is useful.

Daughter: Of course!

St. Peter: Then I should like to hear more evidence of this kind . . . Go on!

Daughter: I remember: My father spoiled me and loved playing games with me. As I grew older, there were conflicts and differences of opinion, but we never really grew apart. The early years had been so good . . .

Sometimes he'd come to my room in his overcoat to kiss me goodnight as I lay sleeping. He liked kissing me when I was little, and I'll never forget his tenderness.

Here's another letter I've saved! It says:

"Thank you for not forgetting your little papa. I'm all right. I'm well, but I miss you. Did you get the peaches and apples? I'll send some more if you order me to. Good-bye, then. I give you a big kiss."

Signed — your Little Papa

St. Peter: I will put it in his file. . . . My, it's a large file! . . . What was the cause of your later separation? It seems to have been very important.

Daughter: The War!

I was fifteen when the War started. It was the events of the War, the tension and crises, that came between me and my father. We took our separate paths.

But I shall never forget his affection, even in the difficult years. He didn't nag or find fault with me. His guidance as a parent was never harsh: that I should study hard, be out in the fresh air as much as possible, and that I ought not to be spoiled.

Yet, of course, I am spoiled.

St. Peter: A father cannot do everything. We blame too much our parents — for what we ourselves have done. . . .

Did others love him?

Daughter: Nowadays, when I read or hear somewhere that my father was mean and cruel, it amazes me that people who knew him well can say such a thing. With all his faults, he was a loyal and generous man. He didn't care for fame, or wealth, or adulation. He was a kind father — and I loved him.

St. Peter: All of us have small sunny corners that we can remember and draw strength from always, through all of life's sufferings. Even those who are callous and cruel retain somewhere, hidden from others, such pockets of goodness in the depths of their souls. I have seen it often!

Daughter: I, too, was taught that the good can triumph over everything. I still believe. . . .

But why does it frequently happen too late — after the very best people have been judged unjustly, senselessly, without pity or compassion?

St. Peter: Again, it is not for me to decide who served the cause of good and who that of vanity and vain-glory. I am only the keeper of the records. It is for another to decide — a higher authority.

Do you have anything else to add?

Daughter: No. . . .

Just a personal comment.

St. Peter: What is it? . . . Go on!

Daughter: Only my own faith that the good will never die; that it lives on in the hearts of people even in the darkest times; that it is hidden where no one thinks to look for it;

that it never disappears completely;

and that everything on our tormented earth that is alive and breathes, that blossoms and bears fruit, lives only by virtue of, and in the name of truth and good.

St. Peter: It will be recorded. . . .

Is that all?

Daughter: Yes.

St. Peter: Could I have your name?
Daughter: Svetlana.
St. Peter: And your father's name?
Daughter: Joseph.
St. Peter: Yes? . . .
Daughter: Joseph Stalin.
St. Peter: *Joseph Stalin:* Father — Friend — Gardener.
    Good-bye . . . and thank you!
Daughter: Good-bye . . .
St. Peter: Could I have the next witness, please?

Afterword

Afterword
A Sermon on Sermons

I delivered my first sermon over twelve years ago. My head was pounding; my hands were sweating; my knees were knocking; my stomach was churning. And it was still the night before!

The next day, I was advised by a friend to approach the pulpit, pause, and take three deep breaths. It seemed like a good idea. So I approached the pulpit; I paused; I inhaled once and exhaled; I inhaled twice and exhaled; but still being nervous, I decided to take a really deep breath . . . so I inhaled and exhaled a mighty blast — and blew my notes off the pulpit!

It was not that I had never heard a sermon. As an undergraduate, I attended Westminster College in Western Pennsylvania, a Presbyterian school with strong church affiliations. I was required to attend chapel services four times a week, and on Sundays the only opportunity for dating was to attend the Vespers Service. In four years, I listened to approximately two hundred sermons.

> I remember one speaker who dropped his manuscript from the pulpit — and watched helplessly as it burned on the candles below.
>
> I remember another speaker who spilled his glass of water at the beginning of the service — and nervously sipped from an empty glass for an hour.
>
> I remember a frightened student speaker who suddenly lit a cigarette in the pulpit — and even asked a person in the audience for an ash-tray.

But most of the sermons were dull and boring.

It is depressing, given the long history of the art, that so few sermons have been permanently enshrined. In America, "Sinners in the Hands of an Angry God" by Jonathan Edwards; "Unitarian Christianity" by William Ellery Channing; and "The Shaking of the Foundations" by Paul Tillich are all in print. Some of the sermons by Henry Ward Beecher, Phillips Brooks, Peter Marshall, and Harry Emerson Fosdick are classic documents — but hardly a part of our everyday literature. Sadly, no one earns a living through the writing of sermons — not even Jimmy Carter!

As to history, sermons first appeared in their modern form during the period of the Reformation — about four hundred years ago. The increased emphasis on the spoken word was a result of the reaction against what many thought to be the magical and superstitious rites of the Roman Catholic Church. The rise of universities, and the increasing level of education among the laity, contributed to the demand for less ritual and more rational forms of communication.

Consequently, Martin Luther, John Calvin, and the other Protestant reformers eliminated the Mass, introduced the Discourse, and justified the Sermon on the basis of its instructional value. It was a conscious imitation of the university system — even to the extent of replacing the multi-colored gowns of the Catholic priests with the black robes of the learned professors. In orthodox language: "the Body of God" in the Mass was given over to "the Word of God" in the Pulpit.

There were a few excesses. While the reformers pointed to Jesus as their precedent, for example, they did not seem to realize that none of his surviving discourses are more than five minutes in length. Yet the early Puritan divines in America held forth for five, six, and seven hours. The families ate their lunches, the children slept on the floor, people died, and babies were born — as the sermon continued on till the setting of the sun. Surely God is more concise!

In recent years, many declining churches have tried to stimulate membership by de-emphasizing the element of preaching in the worship service. Music, poetry, dance, drama, lecture, and dialogue are now a part of "Experimental" services led by minister and laity. In short, every effort has been made to overcome the Protestant view that the sermon is central to worship — and to concentrate on more visual forms of worship.

Of course, there is a problem. It is a major problem. It lies in the strange but undeniable fact that the sermon is so popular. In a recent survey of liberal Protestants:

> when asked to name the most important reason for their church membership, over eighty per cent named the quality of preaching;

> and when asked to list the most compelling reason for their church attendance, over ninety per cent listed the sermon topic;

> and when asked to identify the most important skill of a minister, over ninety-five per cent identified the ability to speak effectively.

So little has changed since the days of Luther. A healthy church has a strong pulpit. A sick church has a weak pulpit. Whatever else a church might offer — this is a law that is never broken.

Let me hasten to add, however, that it is not a law perpetuated by the clergy. In fact, most ministers find the emphasis on preaching to be a terrible cross to bear. For not only does it prevail over the other important functions of the ministry (counseling, teaching, community action, administration), but it also requires the varied skills of research, writing, public speaking, and defending in the reception line — a versatility seldom found in normal human beings.

What is the purpose of preaching? I remember as a student in homiletics class: the teacher concentrated primarily on the style and technique of the art. Over the years, I have come to doubt the importance of that approach.

> It matters very little whether the sermon is written in long-
> hand, typed in manuscript, spoken from notes, or com-
> pletely memorized.

> It matters very little whether the content is long or short,
> analytical or poetical, theological or historical,
> humorous or somber.

> It matters very little whether the preacher is male or female,
> tall or short, intellectual or emotional, wildly eloquent
> or patiently subdued.

If there are a few helpful hints on the style and technique of preaching, it is still such a personal form of artistic expression that no two great preachers are completely alike.

By far the best analysis of preaching was presented in a series of lectures by Henry Ward Beecher in 1873. He said in part:

> "A preacher is in some degree a reproduction of the truth
> in personal form. The truth must exist in him as a living
> experience, a glowing enthusiasm, an intense reality. If
> one may say so, he digests the truth and makes it per-
> sonal, and then brings his own being to bear upon that
> of his hearers. All true preaching bears the impress of
> the nature of the preacher."

And I agree!

The primary element in a sermon, beyond its instructional value, is the element of personality. For the sermon is a public confession: at times merely a confession of dry academic interests; and at other times a highly personal confession of doubt, weakness, fear; and at still other times a confession of faith in God, history, people. But it is always truth — at least truth strained through the living flesh and churning blood of a single human being.

Last summer I was speaking to a friend I had not seen for several years. She said: "I will always remember the sermon you gave on death in 1970," (I had forgotten) — and she proceeded to quote an entire paragraph from memory. It is a common occurrence with the best and worst of preachers.

A lecture or an essay might be better organized than a sermon — but they lack the subjective testimony, the anecdote, the secret, the sharing.

A book or an article might be more profound than a sermon — but they lack the personal presence, the voice, the nuance, the expression.

A television show or an opera might be more expensive than a sermon — but they lack the essential honesty, the doubt, the ignorance, the frailty.

In the course of our weekly rounds, we are constantly bombarded with news, speeches, advertisements, letters, conversations, editorials, and other forms of communications — utterly devoid of honesty and sincerity. Is this not why the sermon is popular? Is this not why the sermon is remembered? Is this not why the sermon can never be replaced?

Of course, it is good to recognize that a sermon is not the ultimate solution to our problems — nor is preaching the ultimate function in a ministry of love. If they are vital and necessary in the life of the church — it is because they often touch a tender nerve, or evoke a memory of childhood, or stimulate a dormant mind, or awaken a broader sympathy, or reflect a hidden hope, or explore a tiny spot in the cosmos. The real salvation is not in the words — but in the actions in between.

In any event, I have been pleased to submit this collection of sermons to the general reader. It represents a diversity of styles, a paradoxical journey, and all the truth I can presently muster. Since I have estimated that I have 1,043 more sermons to deliver before my retirement in the year 2002 A.D. — I have not tried to present everything in a single book. But I hope it has touched you — somewhere.

Reverend David O. Rankin
San Francisco, California
1978

Notes and References

Notes and References

My own approach to the art of preaching was first defined by Soren Kierkegaard, the great Danish theologian of the 19th Century. It is called "The Confessional Style" — and it involves a high degree of personal reflection, personal experience, and personal commitment. It is heavily autobiographical.

I have written the following section for those interested in this particular style of preaching. It will present the sources of quotations; it will explain the background of many of the sermons; and it will attempt to describe some of the important mechanics of preaching.

Remember: a good preacher is not born. It requires four or five years in the pulpit to develop a personal style — and many more years for improving and perfecting. An appreciation of literature and drama is most helpful, but deep personal introspection and a capacity to detect the needs of others is quite essential. Books on preaching offer only a clue to the mystery of the art.

False Title Page
The quotation is from Henry Nevinson, *Goethe: Man and Poet* (New York: Harcourt, Brace and Company, 1932), p. 38.

The genius of Goethe was in his ability to discover the universal values and patterns in the small, intimate details of his own life. It is the very essence of good preaching.

Preface
Jeanne Whitesell is a freelance writer in Danville, California. She is married to William Whitesell and the mother of Nancy, Ted, and Gail. I met with her for a personal interview. It is much too flattering.

There Was a Child Went Forth
The title poem is from Walt Whitman, "Song of Myself," in the *Oxford Book of American Verse* (New York: Oxford University Press, 1950), p. 279. The title of the sermon, as well as the form and rhythm, have been taken from Walt Whitman,

"There Was a Child Went Forth," in the *Oxford Book of American Verse,* pp. 276-278.

This autobiographical poem was presented while sitting on the steps of the chancel. It is very personal, but, hopefully, not gushingly sentimental. This type of sermon is often more valuable to the preacher than to the congregation. It affords the opportunity to follow the ancient Greek injunction: "Know Thyself." No preaching is effective without self-understanding.

Honor Thy Father

The title poem is from e.e. cummings, "my father moved through dooms of love," in *Complete Poems* (New York: Harcourt Brace Jovanovich Inc. 1972), pp. 520-521.

Too many preachers know the answer to every conceivable question — personal and otherwise. This sermon, delivered on Father's Day, permits a high degree of speculation, while doomed to end in perplexity. It is good to share your personal doubts and lingering questions with the Congregation. For me — it has provided many sermon topics.

I Lost My Faith in Wheaties

The title poem is from Sophia Fahs, "It Matters What We Believe," in *Hymns For the Celebration of Life* (Boston: Beacon Press, 1964), p. 376.

Humor is extremely important to a preacher. Formerly seen as a technique to relax an audience before an important speech, it is now a valuable tool in itself. More than anything, it captures the human frailty of the speaker, and contributes to a deeper relationship with the congregation. Laughter is good worship.

Jock-Strap Theology

The title poem is from William Carlos Williams, "The Descent," in *Selected Poems by William Carlos Williams* (New York: A New Directions Paperbook, 1969), p. 132.

Originally, this was a letter to the San Francisco Board of Education protesting their decision to cut the school athletic budget. It was expanded into a sermon after I had reflected on my own experiences in sports. But the Confessional Style of preaching should not merely relate anecdotes and stories. It should always attempt to seek out the religious meaning — that element behind and within the personal and the mundane which all people share.

A View From the Dump

The title poem is from Arthur Graham, "Meditation," in *73 Voices* (Boston: Unitarian-Universalist Association, 1972), p. 33. The idea for the sermon can be attributed to a similar experience by Loren Eiseley which he records in *The Unexpected Universe* (New York: Harcourt Brace Jovanovich Inc., 1969), Chapter Two. The ecology editorial is from the *Newsletter* of the Rev. Dennis Kuby, Minister of Ecology for the Unitarian-Universalist Association. The insights from another poet are from "The Junk Shop," in *The New Yorker Book of Poems* (New York: William Morrow & Company, 1974), by Henri Coulette. The poetry quoted at the conclusion is W.B. Yeats, "The Circus Animals' Desertion," in *Yeats: A Collection of Critical Essays* (Englewood Cliffs: Prentice-Hall, 1963), p. 90.

My usual practice is to minimize the quotations from others in order to present my own thinking. All too often, the preacher feels compelled to prove scholarship, or compatibility with other geniuses, or the possession of a library. A mistaken notion, it turns a good sermon into a poor essay. If you enjoy quoting others — work for a newspaper.

A Fugitive in My Attic

The title poem is from Karl Shapiro, "The Conscientious Objector," in *Selected Poems* (New York: Vintage Books, 1973), p. 120.

At the time, this was a very difficult sermon to present. Already under investigation, I still felt that I had to be open and honest with the members of the church. Happily, they supported my position. I then used the sermon for a recruiting pamphlet to expand the Underground Railroad. Sermons are powerful instruments — so carry them with a delicate hand.

Confessions of an Anarchist Clergyman

The title poem is from Proudhon, "Carnets," in James Joll, *The Anarchists* (New York: Grosset and Dunlap, 1966), p. 70. The definition of "Anarchos" is taken from George Woodcock, *Anarchism* (New York: The World Publishing Company, 1962), p. 10. The quotation from Ortega y Gasset is from E.F. Schumacher, *Small is Beautiful* (New York: Harper Colophon Books, 1975), p. 79. The quotation on "ideals" is from Carl Schurz, "Address at Faneuil Hall, April 18, 1859" in *Familiar Quotations* (Boston: Little, Brown and Company, 1955), p. 644. The prayer from the Denver Anarchist I have never been able to trace — though it appears to be an adaptation of a Proudhon speech.

Politics in the pulpit is often frowned upon — especially by those with a different political philosophy! One of the advantages of the Confessional Style is that everyone knows in advance that I speak only for myself. Consequently, I have never had serious objections. If you are feeding the thirst and hunger of people in other realms, the political sermon will be more readily accepted. Consciously plan to mix your sermon topics — for the flavor and diversity an independent group of people demand.

We Are Cain's Children

The title poem is from Edward Frost, "What Is God?" in *73 Voices* (Boston: Unitarian-Universalist Association, 1972), p. 25. The cartoon is by Charles Schultz and found in Robert Short, *The Gospel According to Peanuts* (Richmond: John Knox Press, 1965), p. 46. The quotation from Sigmund Freud is "Civilization and Its Discontents, in *Great Political Thinkers* (New York: Rinehart and Company, 1956), p. 831. One of the best books on the transition from pre-humans to *homo sapiens* is William Golding, *The Inheritors*.

This is a good example of a sermon which requires rapid and frequent changes of mood. It is therefore necessary to work diligently with the language modulation, the pauses between sections, the facial expressions and the body movements. I normally allow for two hours of concentrated rehearsal prior to Sunday morning. (If you are wondering about total time for sermon preparation, I average about 16 hours per week.)

Confessions of a Unitarian Christian

The title poem is from Soren Kierkegaard, "Training in Christianity," in Carl Michalson, *The Witness of Kierkegaard* (New York: Association Press, 1960), p. 113. The Biblical quotation is *Matthew* 25: 35-37. The perceptive reader will note that I owe a tremendous debt to Kierkegaard. "Confession," "despair," "suffering," "paradox," "witness," and many other key words are central to my theology. He has been a constant companion for the past twenty years.

It is no more difficult to have a conservative theology in a liberal church — than to have a liberal theology in a conservative church. It is important in either case not to use the pulpit as an oppressive instrument against those who think differently. The "I'll get you!" attitude is a ticket to disaster.

Is the Reaper Really Grim?

The title poem is from Rabindranath Tagore, "I Have Got My Leave," in *Gitanjali* (New York: Macmillan Company, 1915), p. 85. The poetry includes: William Shakespeare, *Julius Caesar*; Henry Longfellow, *The Reaper and the Flowers*; Conrad Aiken, *And in the Human Heart*; Alan Seeger, *I Have a Rendezvous With Death*; and the poem on the dead child is by X.J. Kennedy, "On a Child Who Lived One Minute," in *The New Yorker Book of Poems* (New York: William Morrow & Company, 1974), p. 506. I have benefitted from the insights of Elisabeth Kubler-Ross, *On Death and Dying* (New York: Macmillan Company, 1969).

I have experimented with different kinds of sermons on death, because most are either too abstract or too depressing for a Sunday morning audience. The three ingredients here: real situations, poetry, and humor — seem to be a proper mixture. The sermon led to a Seminar on death and dying which was attended by sixty people in two series of sessions. Always be alert in the reception line for needs that might flow out of a particular topic.

The Resurrection

The title poem is from Albert Schweitzer, *The Quest of the Historical Jesus* (New York: The Macmillan Company, 1961), p. 403.

I presented this sermon on Easter Sunday. I greatly enjoy writing historical fiction and I use it frequently as another sermon form. It not only allows for some license with the material, but it also relates ideas and concepts in a medium that is often more enjoyable to the listener. A story is a parable — more easily remembered than a score of facts and striking each person in a wildly different place. The O. Henry ending is the result of my liking O. Henry.

Should I Swim to Honolulu?

The title poem is from T.S. Eliot, "The Dry Salvages," in *Collected Poems* (New York: Harcourt, Brace & World Inc., 1970), p. 198. The quotation from *The Diary* of James Boswell is from Jane Jacobs, *The Death and Life of Great American Cities* (New York: A Vintage Book, 1961), p. 143. Another classic on the subject is Mitchell Gordon, *Sick Cities* (Baltimore: Penguin Books, 1963).

This was an actual letter I wrote in response to a young woman who wanted help and advice before moving to San Francisco. I have since used it as a form letter reply to other inquiries. Every sermon has more than a single purpose. On this particular Sunday, for example, I was responding to a letter, describing my feelings about San Francisco, trying to put the contradictions of the city into a meaningful perspective, saying good-bye to the congregation for the Summer — and perhaps you can find other themes. A listener will always find things you never imagined while writing. Beware!

A Dead Soldier Looks at the War

The title poem is from Archibald Macleish, "The Young Dead Soldiers," in *Hymns For the Celebration of Life* (Boston: Beacon Press, 1964), p. 366.

Another piece of fiction, it was first delivered in the very early years of the Vietnam War. I presented it on a Christmas Sunday, and it was later published as a pamphlet by the Boston Public Library in response to many requests. In preparing a sermon, I aim for good writing, understatement, and subtlety — rather than sudden inspiration, pulpit-pounding, and gross statistics. I prefer to sneak up on people and surprise them.

In the Beginning . . . God

The title poem is from Robert Browning, "The Inn Album," in *Familiar Quotations* (Boston: Little, Brown and Company, 1955), p. 574. The cartoon is by Charles Schulz and found in Robert Short, *The Gospel According to Peanuts* (Richmond: John Knox Press, 1965), p. 109. The quotations from Iknaton, Aristotle, Gandhi, and Helen Keller are in *The Universal God*, edited by Carl Hermann Voss (Boston: Beacon Press, 1961), pp. 6, 3, 59, 225. The quotation from Alfred North Whitehead is "Process and Reality," in John B. Cobb Jr. *A Christian Natural Theology* (Philadelphia: The Westminster Press, 1965), p. 169. While Corita Kent is the artist, the author of the words in the posters is Joseph Pintauro, *To Believe in God* (New York: Harper and Row, 1968).

My fourteen year old son was a "confirmed" atheist, with many God questions still coming to the surface. The purpose of this sermon was to take him and the congregation through my own struggle with the question of God. The reader will note that the sermon is written in the classic "Three Point" form. It has an Introduction, three major points, and a Conclusion. It is the easiest form for organizing material, but it can also become extremely boring over forty Sundays.

Old Macdonald Had a Farm

The title poem is from Stephen Spender, "I Think Continually of Those," in *Hymns For the Celebration of Life* (Boston: Beacon Press, 1964), p. 440. The Iowa poet is Michael Dennis Browne, "Iowa," in *The New Yorker Book of Poems* (New York: William Morrow & Company, 1974), p. 343. The quotations from Roswell Garst are taken from our interview in 1963. The two concluding Biblical quotations are from *John* 6: 26 and *Psalms* 136: 25.

The typical holiday sermons, like Christmas, Easter, Thanksgiving, and Fourth of July, pose a special problem. The overall theme is established by the nature of the holiday, and the freedom to create out of nothing is severely limited. In order to avoid the old, the predictable, and the hackneyed, therefore, the preacher must make a special effort in creativity. I delivered this sermon on the Fourth of July, without ever mentioning the holiday.

The President's Wife

The title statement is from Hall Caine, "The Eternal City," in *Familiar Quotations* (Boston: Little, Brown and Company, 1955), p. 757. All of the incidents related, including the quotations of Abraham and Mary Lincoln, are from Ruth Painter Randall, *Mary Lincoln: Biography of a Marriage* (Boston: Little, Brown and Company, 1953), pp. 1-444.

I have used the pertinent information from a marvelous biography as a parable for the liberation of women. In writing the parable, I had to be sure that the pace was relentless, leading to the inevitable conclusion. In presenting the parable, I chose to use the style of a television commentator — clear, direct, and dispassionate. It was much like a memorial service for all of the women who have suffered throughout the centuries.

A Word For Love And Affection

The title poem is from Emily Dickinson, "If I can stop one heart from breaking," in *The Poems of Emily Dickinson* (Boston: Little, Brown and Company, 1930), p. 5. Other sources included

Gordon Allport, *The Nature of Prejudice* (New York: Doubleday Anchor Books, 1958) and Dennis Altman, *Homosexual Oppression and Liberation* (New York: Avon Books, 1973).

This is an oddity — for me. The sermon was delivered, without notes, while sitting on a stool in the middle of the chancel. It illustrates the advantages of speaking without a manuscript (intimacy, informality, and spontaneity), and also the disadvantages (poor grammar, repetition, and getting lost). Since I feel that the congregation is entitled to my best thoughts, I do not often speak off the top of my head. Those who feel otherwise (a la Fosdick) should remember that he wrote a manuscript, broke it down into paragraphs, memorized the salient points, and then appeared in the pulpit as a preacher inspired by the Holy Spirit. If you have the time — it is a good technique.

See America First

The title poem is from Katherine Lee Bates, "America, the Beautiful," in Richard Charlton MacKenzie (ED.) *Best Loved Poems* (New York: Permabooks, 1951), p. 149. The quotation from Stephen Vincent Benet is "American Names," in the *Oxford Book of American Verse* (New York: Oxford University Press, 1950), p. 948. The song by Woody Guthrie, "Pastures of Plenty," is from *The Other America* by Michael Harrington (Baltimore: Penguin Books, 1965), pp. 51-52.

I was inspired by the work of Michael Harrington to write this epic poem on America. The mixture of love and hate, anger and acceptance, militance and pure delight — is supposed to represent my own feelings while journeying through the contradictions called "America." Delivered on the Fourth of July, it followed by two months my call for the impeachment of President Richard Nixon. While the congregation (and the Press) preferred the impeachment sermon, this was my favorite. So know your own standards and do not confuse them with popular opinion.

The Miracles of Easter

The title poem is from Carl Sandburg, "The People Will Live On," in the *Oxford Book of American Verse* (New York: Oxford University Press, 1950), p. 601. The Biblical quotation at the conclusion is from Jesus in *John* 16: 20.

The five sections of this sermon were presented on Easter Sunday. While organ music and congregational hymns divided each section, dance and responsive readings could also be used. It is extremely important, as the services become more sophisticated, that the sanctuary and the equipment be thoroughly checked. Do it yourself. My lectern collapsed during the third section!

A Sort of Christmas Story

The title prayer is from a street kid, "All By Myself," in Carl F. Burke (ED.) *Treat Me Cool, Lord* (New York: Association Press, 1968), p. 23. The concluding poem is a combination of T.S. Eliot, "Ash-Wednesday," and "Dry Salvages," in *Collected Poems* (New York: Harcourt, Brace and World Inc., 1970), p. 88 and p. 199.

Often, a holiday service will include special music, dance, or ceremonies that shorten the time for a sermon. It is a real test of the preacher's writing skill, for it demands a tight construction and a memorable impact. In this sermonette, I have resorted to the true short-story format. But the dancers were lovely.

My Name is Judas Iscariot

The title words are from Juan Jimenez, "Judas," in *Indictments and Invitations*, Robert L. Cope (ED.), (Boston: Council of Liberal Churches, 1959), p. 95. I much appreciated the portrayal of Judas in Nikos Kazantzakis, *The Last Temptation of Christ* (New York: A Bantam Book, 1960).

Another approach in the Confessional Style is to step into another character. It requires more dramatic ability than straight historical fiction, but it is also more challenging to write and perform. I find it useful for relieving the tedium of the typical sermon. Here, the reader will note, a dramatic change occurs when Judas concludes his special pleading and confronts the audience with his own religious message. Having appeared in the pulpit as e.e. cummings, Charlie Brown, T.S. Eliot, Groucho Marx, and many other characters, I have discovered a freedom of movement and commentary which is normally limited by the boundaries of my own personality. In essence: it is the confession of another character.

Oglethorpe P. Bushmaster of Punxsatawney, Pennsylvania

The title poem is from J. David Scheyer, "Prayer," in *73 Voices* (Boston: Unitarian-Universalist Association, 1972), p. 61. One of the best studies of W.C. Fields is a book by Robert Lewis

Taylor, *W.C. Fields: His Follies and Fortunes* (New York: The New American Library, 1967). I have also seen all of his films, with a special preference for *The Bank Dick*.

Another parable, it followed a grueling week of counseling in which people seemed to be complaining about all kinds of minor problems. Many sermons will be initiated out of the pastoral function of the ministry. While real names should never be used, the sermon can be a valuable tool for mass counseling. When a person remarks: "I have that problem!" or "How did you know I felt that way?" or "You described my feelings perfectly!" — it is not the result of ESP. Rather, I have simply taken the situations I have experienced in counseling — and converted them into sermonic material. Usually, a particular malaise is shared by many people.

I Remember Papa

The title words are from William Shakespeare, "As You Like It," in *Familiar Quotations* (Boston: Little, Brown and Company, 1955), p. 159. The idea for the dialogue originated from Svetlana Alliluyeva, *Twenty Letters to a Friend* (New York: Harper and Row, 1967), pp. 1-235. Svetlana's descriptions of her father and the letters received from him are presented in *Twenty Letters to a Friend.* The quotation from St. Peter on fear is from Hugh Walpole, "The Old Ladies," in *Familiar Quotations*, p. 930.

After reading Svetlana Alliluyeva's book, I was greatly impressed by her steadfast refusal to condemn her father, even though she had just recently emigrated from the Soviet Union. It was a fascinating example of how good and evil are influenced by personal perspective. It is important in the presentation to have St. Peter constantly recording his notes as the daughter is speaking, and to break an old Broadway rule by having the daughter's back to the congregation. After the service, I was told that the dialogue helped many people to better understand and appreciate their own parents.

Afterword

Some of the best theories and examples of preaching can be found in William Channing, *The Works of William E. Channing* (Boston: American Unitarian Association, 1886); Paul Tillich, *The Shaking of the Foundations* (New York: Charles Scribner's Sons, 1948); Harry Emerson Fosdick, *The Living of These Days*, (New York: Harper and Brothers, 1956); and the quotation on preaching is from Henry Ward Beecher, *Yale Lectures on Preaching* (New York: J.B. Ford Company, 1873), p. 4. An excellent work.

Since preaching is an art form, there can be no formula for success. My own Confessional Style relies heavily on personal experience, humor, drama, paradox, and the unexpected; but other styles are equally valid. Besides, after the research, the drafting, the writing, the rehearsal — and just before I enter the pulpit on Sunday morning — I always pray. So perhaps it is the prayer, and not the style, that really sees me through.

AMEN!

The photographs in this book
are the work of Virginia Rankin